1866-1991

125th

ANNIVERSARY

Driftwhistler

Also by Tom Shachtman

BEACHMASTER

WAVEBENDER

Tom Shachtman

DRIFTWHISTLER
A Story of Daniel au Fond

Henry Holt and Company · *New York*

First edition
Published by Henry Holt and Company, Inc.,
115 West 18th Street, New York, New York 10011.
Published simultaneously in Canada by Fitzhenry & Whiteside Ltd.,
195 Allstate Parkway, Markham, Ontario L3R 4T8.

Library of Congress Cataloging-in-Publication Data
Shachtman, Tom.
Driftwhistler : a story of Daniel au Fond / by Tom Shachtman.
Summary: At the head of a band of thirteen different species
of sea mammals, Daniel the sea lion seeks to fulfill a legend and
find Pacifica, the long-drowned, ancient home cove of their race.
Sequel to "Wavebender."
ISBN 0-8050-1285-0
[1. Sea lions—Fiction.   2. Marine mammals—Fiction.   3. Fantasy.]
I. Title.
PZ7.S329Dr   1992
[Fic]—dc20   91-3868

Printed in the United States of America
on acid-free paper.⊗

10 9 8 7 6 5 4 3 2 1

Iceberg melt and mountain fly,
Death in a flower soon must lie,
When Pacifica, by evening star,
Greets the wavebender from afar. . . .

from the legend of Beachmaster Saul

Representatives of the
Thirteen Tribes of the
Descendants of Saul
Who Journey to Pacifica

Daniel au Fond, sea lion
Percival, dolphin
Glex, red-brown harbor seal
Wenceslas, walrus
Porphyry, baleen whale
Popocatepetl, otter
Vaz, northern dappled seal
Nezan, elephant seal
Esmeralda, polar bear
Lavender, killer whale
Cendrillon, manatee
Fitzwilliam, narwhal
        and, that of the lost tribe,
Siwaga, leopard seal

Contents

Driftwhistler

Part One

GATHERING
THE TRIBE

1

The Rainbow
and the Cloud of Night

*I*t was a familiar dream, one that came to sea lion Daniel au Fond often on those nights when the moon was a slender silver tooth: He was in the depths, battling the ultimate enemy. This time, Kratua was a thousand-headed worm whose tongues caused the ocean to boil, with a crackling, tearing sound. Daniel squirmed, and suddenly his flippers detached themselves and became sturdy swimmers; his whiskers flew out as swift penetrators, his jaw filled with gleaming edges ready to do his bidding: He was more than himself, he was a whole tribe of animals. What was hot, the tribe cooled; what was in the way, they bypassed or overwhelmed. Daniel was all-powerful—yet also terrified that this enormous power would turn him to sand. Firebreath opened his mouth and spewed out slanting red rays that beat at the lids of Daniel au Fond's eyes.

The dream faded, and in the early morning sun Daniel awoke. He was safe; he was not yet sand. Groggy, he clambered with his flippers three lengths above the water's edge to the highest rock of the small island to get a sense of the day. They were a thousand lengths from the shore of the continent to the east; to the west there were no other islands. When he reached the pinnacle, Daniel saw a rainbow—not in the sky, where rainbows usually appeared, but below him, spread out on the surface of the ocean to the west. Was it real or a part of his dream?

Unlike skyborne rainbows, this one shimmered on the waters in swirls of purple and gold and orange and green, elegant patterns that stretched out toward the western horizon. He barked for Anna to come up on the high rocks and share the strange rainbow with him. During the night, her coat had dried to the bronzed shade he had always loved.

"How beautiful," Anna whispered.

"A sight this lovely and unexpected must be important," he said to Anna. "Where did it come from? What is it telling us?"

"The shelf," Anna murmured, pointing at the metal icon of the bipeds barely visible a thousand lengths to the west. "It's different, now. Twisted."

Yesterday, on their way north, they had passed the biped thing, a shelf resting atop metal legs. From the island, though, even Daniel's sharp eyes could not make out how the biped ledge had changed. "Something must have happened to it during the dark tides," Anna murmured, shouldering closer.

Anna's notion brought back a fragment of the dream that had troubled Daniel as he slept: a cracking, wrenching sound. It mingled with present noises: faint biped voices that came to him on the wind, and the heavy, beating throb of a biped airfloater that seemed to be heading for the twisted shelf. Daniel now realized that the dazzling, seaborne rainbow covered only that part of the sea between the shelf and the island.

On the rocks that served as sleeping perches, other members of the tribe stirred at the airfloater's passage, but did not immediately react to the rainbow. Daniel hopped down from the peak to ask why, and discovered that at sea level the startling colors on the waters could not be properly seen. How odd! At the island's edge, one-cycle pups played happily with small crabs and crayfish in seaweed-slick tide pools. The island teemed with life, most of it encased in very small shells.

Aloft, near the broken shelf, several biped airfloaters swooped and dipped like so many albatrosses around a fresh fish kill. Their unmistakable clamor woke the remainder of the sea mammals of Daniel's tribe. The sun's red rays became gold-white—and the rainbow vanished completely. By the time the rest of the tribal members had stretched and yawned their sleep away, the shimmering sight was gone, and in its place on the surface of the sea were patches of brownish-black color bobbing with the waves. As Daniel watched, two patches met and flowed together to become a single ugly blob on the sea and then rose onto the outer rocks of the small island, where the next wave could not wash it off.

It was the time of day for pinnipeds to soak up some sun. In the past few days, while the moon had shed her coat, gone through the dark nights, and emerged with a quarter of a new coat, the tribe had traveled many thousands of lengths. Moreover, last evening's hunting had not resulted in full bellies for any of the members, not for

Daniel, the other sea lions, and the seals, nor for Wenceslas the walrus, Percy the dolphin, or Porphyry the whale. The tribe would need to warm themselves and regain their strength so they could hunt again. That was why Daniel was not initially alarmed by the first ugly blob of ooze, and did not miss Porphyry or Percival. The latter two tribal members, unable to beach, slept at sea; he thought they must be off hunting somewhere. Only when blackened, belly-up, opaque-eyed fish began to float against the outer rocks did Daniel realize that daybreak's shimmering vision was actually a rainbow of death.

The hake were coated with a muck the color of the darkest earth that could stick to fur and even burn through; old encounters with the muck had left Daniel's coat with some nearly bald spots.

A flock of noisy, excited sea gulls descended on the dead fish as if they had just found that greatest of treasures, a meal that had taken no effort to hunt. They pecked and tore at the blackened fish with great glee, and filled the air with territorial screams and warnings to the sea-lion tribe to keep away. Fortunately, Daniel's charges knew enough not to eat such dead fish. He barked the tribe toward the sea. Individuals and pairs slipped off the rocks, eluded the wildly pecking birds, and entered the foaming surf. First in was Goshun, the almost-grown son of Daniel and Anna. Goshun was followed by his mate Filomena, daughter of the dappled seals Agwah and Meeyon, who also traveled with the tribe. Several more dappled and red-brown seals leaped in, along with the big sea-lion cows Zelda and Marlena and their pups. Then came Parduk, Daniel's ad-olescent daughter, followed by the bulky walrus, Wenceslas. As usual, bringing up the rear was Daniel's old father, Tashkent, the grizzled whitefur who was the tribe's Whistler.

Daniel looked around for Percival and Porphyry, who still had not returned. He couldn't wait for them now. Pounded by the action of the waves against the island's outer rocks, the floating muck had become small, slimy balls. Daniel headed the tribe west. Once away from the waves that frothed at the island's shore, Daniel could see that patches of the stuff alternated with areas of open water. Toward the horizon, the way seemed clear. He gave the order to dive and to stay down. As he pushed below the surface, Daniel's nostrils and the back of his mouth closed, so he was no longer in danger of accidentally swallowing any of the stuff that he might happen to swim through. His eyes widened, adjusting to semidarkness. The sun's rays were not reaching very far down today; in midmorning, they gave no more light than at dusk. Above, the surface over him became covered more and more with black ooze, clear only where swirling, eddying surface waves kept the intruding stuff at bay. He had planned to stay under until the tribe got past the twisted metal shelf and into open waters. With each dozen flipper thrusts, however, the darkness above seemed more continuous. Daniel shook off gestured suggestions that they go up to breathe; their stored air could last for some time, and Daniel did not want anyone's nostrils or mouth befouled, as would surely happen if they surfaced for air.

The claws of a great black lobster reached toward them. Daniel was startled until he realized it was only tendrils of the ooze beneath the surface, twisted, swirled, and buffeted by undersea currents. Daniel dodged the claws and kept on. But the next thing he saw made him slow his pace: Fifty lengths ahead, an intense blackness billowed from the sea floor, a flowing, steadily enlarging night so intense that he could not pierce it with his eyes; it threatened to envelop him and the tribe completely.

Fear clenched Daniel's throat. He backed away and forced himself to think. This must be the birthplace of the ooze; from here it must issue and slowly rise. The wall was not a barrier of stone or coral but a cloud of blackness he dared not enter because he might never emerge from it alive.

Au Fond. To the bottom! He must get below the stuff. Daniel dove down twenty lengths and neared the sea floor. A gust of current blew the ooze aside for a moment and he glimpsed a huge metal worm sticking straight up from the bottom. It was broken, and a stream of the ooze emerged from its jagged mouth. This was the lower part of the biped shelf. The opening clouded over, and there was nothing but billowing, bubbling night suffusing through the waters. He scraped sand, but could find no passageway under or around the blackness. The cloud wall massed in front of him, hundreds of lengths in each direction and moving toward him.

There was no fighting this ooze, and no easy route to avoid it. The tribe would have to flee in the only direction available to them—back toward the island. He turned tail, and saw as he headed away from the cloud of night that the frightened questions in the eyes of his tribe yielded to relief.

"Some wavebender I am," Daniel muttered to himself

as the tribe coursed east. A cycle ago, when Daniel had organized a line of whales in front of Silent Turtle Island to protect it from a tidal wave, Percival the dolphin had given to him this title, which meant a being who could counter great natural forces. Now Daniel felt helpless to do anything about the ooze that had almost caused the surface above the swimmers to disappear.

As in his dream, Daniel was now aided by more than himself. The northern dappled seals hunted beneath ice packs during the moons of ice in their home seas, and were trained to locate distant breathing holes. Under the ooze there were still occasional patches of light. Agwah took over as search leader for Daniel and soon found an open patch. The youngsters breathed through it first, grateful for the fresh air, then the smaller seals and sea-lion cows, and last of all the sea-lion bulls.

In the vicinity of the small island whence they had earlier fled, Daniel avoided the most inviting landing place, where the rocks were flat and the tide pools full of food, and circled instead to the multiple rocks and crags that made the water foam with treacherous passage; here, he believed, would be the least ooze. "If any gets on you, don't lick at your fur," Daniel yelled, and moved ashore. The bodies of blackened birds and fish littered every rock in the area where they had slept last night; most were dead, but a few birds still stirred, some jerkily, others with an exaggerated slowness, their wings and legs and beaks clogged. Moss-green rocks and reflecting tide pools had not entirely disappeared, but were so thickly covered with black slime that they seemed only contours of darkness. In them, no living creature moved. Daniel's mind reeled, trying to understand the rainbow death. Even sharks who never stopped moving ceased to kill after gorging; but this ooze did not stop coming on. The sound of the water had changed; now the blackened waves that rose at the island's shore made a slurping, slow noise, horrible to hear. Only the waves' ceaseless, gliding movement told him that this was still the sea.

Was this the start of the ultimate disaster warned of in the sea lions' legends? The verses foretold a possible catastrophe that could mean the end of all the oceans. How swiftly and unexpectedly the destruction of the seas seemed to be approaching!

"We can't stay here much longer," Goshun said.

"You're right about that, my son. The question is which direction to pursue," Daniel responded. Other days, he and Goshun had their disagreements; not now. Together they searched the horizons. Less muck could be seen on the waters to the east.

"So: We go to the land of the bipeds?" Goshun asked bitterly. Once he had been captured by bipeds, and had been so badly treated by them that he hated every being that walked on two legs. Daniel had been captured, too, once, but his experience hadn't been so awful. Nonetheless, Daniel knew the dangers of associating with bipeds. He had struggled to maintain his tribe without becoming dependent on a home cove along these shores that had become so completely infested with the two-legged land-goers. Even a thousand lengths from shore, the bipeds' domination of the land was obvious: A dense pall of cloud overlay the areas to north and south where biped dwellings crowded cliffs and beaches. To approach the continent meant courting danger, but to let the ooze overtake them meant certain death. "When there's no other way, the decision is easier," Daniel said.

Goshun shrugged his massive mane and shoulders, but went along as, reluctantly but firmly, Daniel urged the tribe back into the foaming surf and led them toward the continental shore. For a quarter-tide they aimed for an area of high cliffs and churning surf, rather than for a sandy beach; bigger rocks usually meant fewer bipeds.

On their way to the continent, the tribe passed two unusual sights. The first was a half-dozen large biped floaters of the sort that routinely hunted salmon, floaters with their nets furled, rocking atop befouled waves while under them swam frightened schools of salmon. Daniel wondered if the bipeds were letting the salmon swim away so the fish would not be hurt by the ooze on the waters. The second appeared in a current swirl near the base of a cresting wave: a bewildered otter with a freshly killed salmon in his mouth. His eyes bulged and his fur was twisted with ooze. He had strayed too far out into the currents in pursuit of his favorite food; now, his fur soaked heavy with black stuff, he was unable to beach.

One couldn't directly offer assistance to these small cousins, for that generally piqued their pride. But Daniel had to do something. "Bit of a strong current, this tide," he said to the floundering otter.

"Yah. Hard swim," the otter barked out in three gasps; the speech made him drop the salmon, which immediately drifted off. Daniel casually nudged the fish back toward him. Having thus demonstrated his good intentions, he then offered gently to allow the otter to beach with the tribe. The little one nodded gratefully. Daniel had some of the bulls surround and protect him from the force of the waves as the tribe swam for shore.

Full long tide: That was good, for the next low would allow the waters to recede, leaving more beach for sea lions. His flippers touched pebbles and he galloped out onto rounded rocks, a bit of sand, and occasional boulders. Daniel had hoped to find the shore clear of the ooze, but some was already there, clinging to the rocks, its odor assaulting his nostrils. He shoock off excess water, but could not rid himself of the piercing smell.

"Can we ride surf, Daniel?" Parduk said, her eyes glistening with excitement. Several moons had passed since the younger members of the tribe had had such fun, for the southern oceans were more calm than these; it took a steep underwater escarpment near landfall and a sizable surface wind to produce the best conditions for shooting along the curl of the waves.

"Too much ooze in the water," he answered, explaining that he did not want their fur to become further befouled. The younger members were annoyed, but they obeyed. The otter, Uxmal, shivered and curled up in a ball. Struggling to breathe, he gasped that he had come from a kelp bed just north of this part of the coast.

As the waters receded, mussels and other shelled creatures that usually clung to the seaweed and rocks were revealed, dead, dripping with the black stuff. Daniel loped along on the stones, avoiding those entirely covered with slime, toward a dozen gaping shells of abalone, their rich multicolored insides glinting with the rays of the declining sun. Abalones' muscles were so strong that when healthy they were able to resist the usual sea-mammal practice of smashing bivalves on rocks in order to open the shells and eat their innards. But these were dead, and their shells were open.

"Did the ooze kill them, Daniel?" Anna asked, coming near.

"It must have. Not even a good-sized storm would roll this many onto an isolated beach."

"Daniel, I'm frightened."

"So am I. So is everyone," he replied.

"You must find Pacifica soon," she whispered.

There it was again: Pacifica, the goal that had eluded Daniel au Fond ever since he had become aware of the power of the old legend. A fragment of the legend warned that if the sea lions did not discover the long-drowned, ancient home cove of the race, and learn its secrets, the oceans would die. For countless generations the alarm had been sung, but only in Daniel's time did the destruction seem imminent. Pacifica must be found—and soon.

Tashkent lumbered up. "We must hold the ceremony now," he said, gruff as always. Daniel agreed. Accompanied by the shivering, ooze-covered Uxmal, the members of the tribe arranged themselves to look west, out toward the horizon, gazing silently until the sea bit the sun and spilled its bloodlight onto the waters and the clouds. Only when the last red rays had entirely vanished did Tashkent raise aloft his vibrant and compelling voice to lead the song about the ancient home cove of all sea mammals:

> *"Deep, the realm of Beachmaster Saul,*
> *Great-great-grandfather of us all;*
> *Dark, Pacifica's storied walls,*
> *Yet still the monarch sounds his call:*
> *'Come, lions that dwell in the sea,*
> *We travel far in mystery.' "*

In the early days of the world, Pacifica had been home to both bipeds and sea lions, a beautiful place where the two warm-blooded races of mammals lived in harmony. Then the sea-lion race's founder, Beachmaster Saul, was betrayed by the main biped, Kanonah. It happened when the rains sank Pacifica. Unable to swim, Kanonah begged Saul to carry him in his belly until land reappeared. Saul did—but then the two-legged stole Saul's female, the Great Mother Selchie, taking her to live on land with him. Saul could not go home again because Pacifica had drowned. Ever since, his descendants, the thirteen tribes of sea mammals, had roamed the seas. Sea lions, seals, walruses, and their cousins still yearned for their ancient home cove. But Pacifica would not be found, the legend said,

> *Until the spirit of Saul returns,*
> *Until the wave is bent and burns,*
> *Until the sun in darkness dwell,*
> *Until Kanonah's pups do sea lions tell.*

Astonishingly, these conditions had already been partially met. Daniel had demonstrated by his actions the spirit of the Great Beachmaster. He had built on Bird's Neck Isle in the far north an icon of Beachmaster Saul that protected from harm the white-coated infant seals of the dappled tribe. He had formed this unusual tribe of seals, sea lions, a walrus, a dolphin, and a whale. And under his direction, just a cycle ago, an enormous tidal wave had been slowed, if not entirely "bent," by Daniel's arranging of the whales in its path, after which the red tide had "burned" up in the heat of the sun. Two unfulfilled conditions of the verse continued to puzzle Daniel. How could the sun ever live in darkness? And when would Kanonah's pups ever talk to the pups of Saul—"do sea lions tell," as the ancient verse put it. The bipeds were seldom friendly to sea lions, and the two races seemed to have no language in which they could communicate. Despite these unanswered questions, Daniel continued to be a prisoner of hope; someday, Pacifica would be found.

The singers began what had become for Daniel the most exciting verse of the legend, one that named the time and place for future action.

> *"Iceberg melt and mountain fly,*
> *Death in a flower soon must lie,*
> *When Pacifica, by evening star,*
> *Greets the wavebender from afar;*
> *Then shall warmbloods be not cold*
> *To ancient secrets that unfold.*
> *Then shall seagoers cease to fear*
> *The wrath of Kanonah coming near!"*

This verse raised hopes that Pacifica's secrets could be learned, that peaceful coexistence with the bipeds might be reestablished. But the last lines also voiced that terrible warning to which Anna recently alluded:

"But should the tide pool still not clear,
The very oceans shall disappear."

Night itself had washed over the beach, Daniel thought, and had also covered the moon. He had to remind himself that this was the middle of that period of thirteen tides that came thirteen times each cycle during which the moon did not show herself. The stars seemed unable to pierce through the clouds to give their relief to the darkness. There would be no twinkling outline of Beachmaster Saul above them, this night. Unable to sleep, Daniel lay on a rock. He was happy for his tribe's escape from the black ooze. But he felt in his bones that the prophecy of wide destruction was dangerously near to coming true. He must find and fathom the secrets of Pacifica quickly, or else be the last beachmaster of the sea lions the oceans would ever know.

2

Beach of the Two Suns

*D*ark above, dark below on the beach, and the powerful ooze smell that masked all others kept Daniel from noticing the arrival of bipeds until they were within a few lengths. Then, the fur on the back of his neck bristling with alarm, he barked the tribe awake. It was just before dawn. A few upright creatures, covered in green and with white clamshells over their noses and mouths, went about the landing place dropping the remains of dead birds into large black nets. Others, holding worm-shaped rolls of flat, white kelp, tried to wipe the black mess away, one rock at a time.

How silly a thing, Daniel thought; each new crest of leap tide brought more ooze; shortly, rocks cleansed by the bipeds would again be covered with muck. Why pay more attention to rocks than to the crabs, mussels, and other life-forms on the beach? He would never understand bipeds. There was a loud noise from the western horizon. He turned and saw what seemed a second sun but was actually a fire at the biped shelf.

For a quarter-tide, bipeds wandered about the landing place, dabbing at the rocks with their white kelp. The black smoke from the blazing shelf drifted nearer. Would the waters be covered with fire? Daniel shuddered, recalling Kratua, the monster that guarded long-drowned Pacifica, whose breath was supposed to be aflame. Fire existed in water only in his dreams, didn't it? And there weren't supposed to be two suns, either.

A biped came close to Agwah, but a growl kept the two-legged at a distance. Daniel was proud of his followers for staying away from the bipeds. When Daniel was a pup, a disastrous cyclone had killed many of the sea lions; Tashkent, then the leader of the tribe, had allowed bipeds to rescue the survivors—but at a cost. The sea lions had been forced to live in a cove that stifled many of their natural impulses. It was in reaction to that too-pleasant trap that Daniel had escaped and begun his adventures. Now even Tashkent stayed away from the bipeds, knowing that what came from their hands was a poison worse than that of a stinging jellyfish.

In the lea of a boulder, Uxmal the ooze-covered otter just stared vacantly, his mouth parched and open, his breathing shallow. A pair of bipeds reached down and picked up Uxmal, intending to take him away. The ooze had evidently made him slippery, for, with a burst of effort, Uxmal squirmed out of their arms, fell to the rocks, and scrambled toward water.

"Help me," he moaned. "Get me home! Don't want to die in black net!"

Daniel understood that these particular bipeds were possibly going to try to help the otter—but he also knew that Uxmal was beyond assistance and wanted to go to sand in his own cove. Interposing his body between the little one and the bipeds, Daniel yelled commands. From all about the ooze-covered landing place, the seals, sea lions, and Wenceslas loped toward the water. Daniel fastened his teeth on the loose fur at the otter's neck and carried him the last ten lengths. The shock of the waves revived Uxmal, who began to paddle mightily away from the Beach of Two Suns.

Daniel arranged the tribe in its traditional teardrop-shaped traveling formation, himself in the lead, Anna by his side, the bulls behind him in two curving lines to protect the cows and younger tribal members who swam between them, and Tashkent bringing up the rear. Uxmal soon had to be shouldered above the water by the cows at the center of the formation, Marlena and Zelda. The bulls were too large for this task, as their slightest lurch would have crushed the little otter between them. As the tribe headed north along the coast and the ooze became thinner, Uxmal grew weaker; he now had to ride along on Wenceslas's broad back, holding on with his claws to the bulging folds of the walrus's neck. Daniel searched the western horizon. Where were Porphyry the whale and Percival the dolphin? How would they find the tribe if Daniel turned into the estuary rather than proceeding to the north seas for the birthing season? He closed his eyes and imagined the faces of his two friends to tell them soundlessly of the detour. Percy had told him to try such a communication when all else failed.

Two thousand lengths and a half-tide farther on, the waters themselves began to change. Daniel felt it first as a cooling thrill to his whiskers, then as a taste he could not yet identify, then as a subsurface current of fresh, sweet water. A hundred flipper strokes to the north, they could see the beginning of the wide river and the side channel that became the swampy, reed-filled banks of the estuary. Daniel recognized this area from cycles past as the prime territory of the otters. "Uxmal," he called out. "You're home!" But the ooze-covered cousin could no longer hear him.

~~~~~

Thumpers were at work. These otters were experts at floating on their backs, placing flat rocks on their bellies, and pounding on the rocks clams, mussels, and sea urchins. Breaking the shells, the thumpers prepared food for a feast. Overall, Daniel thought, the otters were marvelous creatures. It was thrilling to see how well the cousins navigated the calm channel and upper estuary, and how they climbed out of brackish water onto muddy banks. Otter scouts had met Daniel and had taken Uxmal's body away for burial in a secret place in the reeds. Daniel noted that the westward flow of the channel and the outward thrust of the main river prevented the ocean ooze from entering this area. Black clouds of smoke still disfigured the western horizon, but in the marsh the declining sun fired the reeds to gold. A glorious setting, except for biped structures that stood on immensely long crab legs above the estuary, topped with metal caves and connected one to another by long kelp lines.

"Like nice reeds, beachmaster?" asked the female otter named Palenque, presenting him with a clump of reed ends that dangled bottom soil. This was evidently an otter delicacy, so Daniel chewed at it politely without comment;

the taste was foul. Exhausted from only a half-day's traveling, he thought that he must be getting old. He had seen nearly as many cycles as there were digits on his foreflippers, and would soon be a grandfather; Filomena was pregnant with his son Goshun's first pup.

Something glittering in the fleshy part of Palenque's ear caught Daniel's eye: metal. It must have been placed there by the bipeds. He recalled from his moons in the bipeds' laboratory that the two-leggeds sometimes clipped animals in this way before releasing them. In the laboratory a set of metal whiskers had even been stuck deep into Daniel's own shoulder; by means of these, the bipeds had tracked him across the ocean, until Tashkent had ripped out the metal whiskers. Daniel wondered whether bipeds were watching the otters from afar, and glanced uneasily up at a tall metal shelf. Inside, there was some movement.

"We have grand feast this evening, beachmaster," the otter cow said, breaking Daniel's mood and causing him to stop staring at the bipeds that he thought he saw in the shadows of the shelf.

"I'm sure we will," Daniel replied. "But where is Popocatepetl?" Daniel and the leader of the otters, nicknamed Popo, had once shared an adventure in a sargasso. Becalmed in the overheated waters, Daniel and Popocatepetl had been attacked by an enormous, crazed beast that had tried to kill everything in its path. Percival the dolphin, Esmeralda the white polar bear, and Lavender the killer whale had also been with them—but at the moment of crisis it was Daniel who had thought up the plan to lure the beast onto a beach, and Popo who had shown great courage in being the lure. They had successfully stranded the monster and left it to die. Later, in the far north, Esmeralda had warned him when seal clubbers were about to attack. And, of course, Percival was now a member of Daniel's own motley tribe.

Where was that confounded dolphin Percival anyway? And Porphyry, the baleen whale? It was fortunate, Daniel thought, that these two flukers were not in the shallows at this moment of lull tide, for they might have beached. As it was, Goshun and Wenceslas had climbed onto a muddy island that served as the base of a biped structure.

"We push it down," Wenceslas boasted, grunting and heaving his weight at a metal leg of the shelf.

"Biped waste," Goshun said, spitting the words out. He lowered his head and butted it as well. "They won't spy on this place."

Daniel swam and humped his way through the matted reeds and low water to where the supporting legs swayed with the bulls' assaults. "This isn't the same sort of shelf as the one that spawned the ooze," he observed. "Why be angry at it?"

"Because it belongs to the bipeds," Goshun shouted.

"If you topple it, you may harm the bipeds inside. And that wouldn't prevent other bipeds from coming into the estuary and putting it back up again. It might even bring the wrath of the bipeds down on the otters."

"Look, Daniel"—Goshun scowled at him—"if I want to do this, that's my concern. The otters aren't objecting."

"You're the size of ten otters. They wouldn't start a fight with you."

Goshun glowered at Daniel. With a start, the beach-master realized that his son had now become fully as large as he. And the bristling fur on younger bull showed no graying hairs. He seemed ready to challenge Daniel, and not inclined to back down from this senseless argument. For several moments father and son stared at each other. Then both heard a chattering, nasal voice.

"Pick on someone your own size, Daniel," challenged the voice. "Like me." Daniel whirled, expecting to see a large creature, and was surprised to find Popocatepetl looking at him from the top of a small mud flat.

"Hello, Popo, old friend. I was trying to reason with my son about—"

"Reason with a son, bully a bull, but don't meddle with Popocatepetl," the otter said, rubbing his nose with a long paw.

"I beg your pardon." Daniel spluttered. He would have said more, but Popo was no longer there to hear. The otter tore around the reed-filled shallows of the estuary making odd faces at Daniel. Popo swerved at the mud pile at the base of the biped shelf, and chattered at Daniel.

"We'll have a race. Get soil on your face," Popo screamed. The entire tribe of otters, lined up on a bank, tittered at the thought.

Should Daniel take up Popocatepetl's challenge, or be dignified and refuse to wrestle in the mud? Looking about the estuary, he sought the eyes of Anna. Settling back on her hind flippers, she seemed to tell him this was a test he must pass, not avoid, so Daniel decided to go ahead.

In a flash, the otter led Daniel on a wild and very muddy chase about the mud piles, reeds, and banks of the shallow area. They constantly had to dodge small obstacles, and to find passageways through rivulets clogged with leaves.

At a clump of reeds, Popo turned suddenly and splashed Daniel. Daniel answered in kind. If this was proper behavior in the territory of the otters, Daniel thought, he'd do his best. But after a while, as Daniel chased Popo, it didn't seem much like fun. Daniel's fur became more and more covered with the muck, which slowed him down. He didn't have the otter's sharp claws and couldn't grasp the reeds or woody cattails to make sharp turns, as Popo did. But when Popo went into slightly deeper waters, in the middle of a side channel, Daniel was pleased. Now he'd catch the little thumper! Daniel lowered himself beneath the water of the narrow channel. The chase had become very serious, and he wanted almost desperately to close his teeth firmly on Popo's tantalizing tail. Suddenly a wall of riverbank appeared in front of Daniel. He barely had time to avoid slamming into it. Daniel put all of his efforts into coming to a stop, and when he recovered enough to continue the chase, he found that Popo was nowhere in sight. Had he gone through the barrier? For that matter, where was the barrier now? It seemed to have become nothing more than a heavy concentration of bottom soil billowing about in the waters. Had the wall been real or not?

"You lose," Popo said gaily from the bank of the channel as Daniel stuck his head above the water. The sea lion was almost entirely covered with bottom mud. "Now the famous Daniel must make for the otters a treasure of what-is-the-matter."

Puzzled, tired, and feeling exceedingly unclean, with his skin itching and his eyes troubled, Daniel was sorry that he had ever brought the dying Uxmal back to his home territory. He was close to being angry at his friend. But Popocatepetl was insistent and smiling, and Anna's eyes urged him to cooperate with the host tribe, so Daniel began to build one of the treasures for which he had become known. Those animals who traveled the oceans along the continent had come to recognize Daniel's creations, made of shells, stone, driftwood, sand, the occasional piece of biped glass that had been thrown ashore by the sea; such treasures dotted the islands up and down the coast between the icy realm of the northern seals and the southern archipelago. Daniel decided to work quickly in order to get the present task finished. Usually, these creations took him quite a while—a whole tide, or, as with the great statue of Saul on Bird's Neck Island, for which he had had the assistance of a dozen bulls, an entire moon quarter. While Popo's laughing eyes watched, Daniel made a design that included mussel and snail shells, reeds, cattails, and bits of driftwood. He discovered as he worked that he could drip bottom mud from his flippers onto the bank in such a way that the wind dried it into an elegantly rising pattern in which to set the curving shells. By the time he was finished, Daniel felt good using the bottom mud in a way he had never considered before; moreover, his anger was gone.

"You win," Popo now said. "Follow me, please." This time there was no chase. Hidden in the marshes now glowing with the sun's last rays of the day was a sweet-water pool that ran fresh and cool. Daniel plunged into it alongside Popo. The sun could barely be seen through the reeds and the banks, but it was the sun again, free of the black clouds that had earlier obscured it. In the secret cleansing pool Daniel felt the muck slide away from his body, felt the itching cease, felt the tiredness evaporate in the tiny bubbles welling up. The world wasn't such a bad place, after all.

~~~~~

The sun had been eaten by the sea, and darkness ruled but for the crescent of new moon. Having feasted on snails, oysters, mussels, clams, sea urchins—Daniel didn't really like the spiny urchins, but nibbled to be polite—the tribes were ranged along a bank at one side of the estuary, enjoying the evening. A chorus of frogs croaked from the reeds, stalked by a lone snowy egret walking through the shallows on its sticklike legs, every now and then impaling a green jumper on its pointed bill. Popocatepetl thanked Daniel formally for enabling the tribe to mingle with the river bottom the body of a member who had died at sea. Daniel, in turn, thanked Popo for shelter from the black ooze now afflicting the outer ocean. There was some general discussion that the waters all over the known world were being soiled by biped filth—the secret bathing place of the otters, Popo said, was the last one they could still use; all the others had become poison.

Then the hosts sang their version of the legend of Beachmaster Saul, ancestor of all thirteen seagoing races of mammals. Otters believed him to have been a small, cunning beast—"Saul the Little," or "Saul the Trickster"—not the enormous pinniped celebrated by the walruses, or the sealion-sized hero that Daniel himself had always imagined as the sire of his line. The otters' verses, and moon's reappearance after her absence of thirteen tides, roused Daniel from his lethargy. He had news for Popo. To introduce it, he sang a verse from the otter's own version of the legend:

"Then rose moon's turtle, who was a riddle,
Full of ways both straight and curved,
Twisting, narrow, broad as the world.
Who can shout the Trickster's words
That let the voice of the turtle be heard?"

"That's our song, flippers long."

"Well, Popo, we found the turtle—and then lost it again," Daniel said. Anna glared at him. "Lost *her* again," he corrected himself.

"Tell more," Popo said. He tried not to betray his mounting excitement, but stopped chewing and humming.

In the course of voyaging through the southern archipelago, Daniel recounted, they had come upon a very large and obviously old turtle. Her shell was "full of ways both straight and curved" that on closer examination revealed one cluster of four small signs: an egg, a double crescent, a snake, and the outline of a turtle. Daniel had not immediately recognized their significance. But when the tribe had arrived in the vicinity of four islands in the archipelago that had the same shapes as the signs on the turtle's back, Daniel had been thunderstruck, and concluded that the turtle they had seen had been the legendary "moon's turtle."

"Ah," said Popo, his posture alert, though his eyes seemed focused far away, as if he were trying to envision the scene himself.

Daniel mentioned that they had seen the turtle a second time. "Well, it wasn't exactly *we* who saw her. It was a quadruped. Sigmund the orangutan, a dear friend of mine, now gone to sand." His eyes misted at the thought of Siggy, who had died on the island.

Anna took over telling the story. "The orangutan mentioned before he died that he had seen the turtle, and that a spot on her shell was fiery red. Evidently, the turtle was unable to stay in that bay because the beach where she wanted to lay her eggs vanished under the great wave."

"We expect the turtle will return to that beach during the twelfth moon of this new cycle," Daniel said, "and we plan to be there to inspect her shell more closely. We should be able to find the exact location of the fiery red spot—which just has to represent Pacifica. It'll give us directions to locating the long-drowned home cove of our race."

Popocatpetl cried, and embraced Daniel. Then he turned to his assembled tribe and announced in a solemn whisper, "Moment we wait for thousand moons has come. Voice of the turtle is heard."

~~~~~

"There are clues all through the legend," Daniel began his explanation as they watched the crescent moon from the weeds along the bank. " '*Dark, Pacifica's storied walls*'— that verse tells us that Pacifica had walls, or at least boundaries, and that it later sank, which implies that it was once on land. Probably an island rather than a continent." Daniel settled back on his hind flippers. "My guess is that it was the sort of place where land and water mingled, where one didn't end abruptly and the other begin—maybe channels through low banks, as you have here, or huge tide pools, or caves in the rocks. A beautiful place, certainly—both races were happy there, and lived in harmony with one another. A place of carefree surf riding, where a sea mammal could do a great deal each day, or nothing at all." Daniel quoted a verse he particularly liked:

> *"In Pacifica did lions and bipeds thrive,*
> *Nor could one without the other live,*
> *Biped and sea lion, hand and flipper*
> *Linked in the jaws of forever.*

"To me, that means the brothers loved one another, surely," Daniel went on enthusiastically, "and they worked together."

Heads were nodding as Daniel continued to speak and make his word picture of what he thought Pacifica had been like. "Fishing," he said: "There would have been plenty of fish and bivalves in the waters nearby. Building statues: There must have been marvelous treasures. Certainly there are tasks the bipeds can do with their hands that we cannot do, but by the same token there are underwater treasures to recover that bipeds cannot reach but that we can. I'm sure both races united against some common enemy . . . coldbloods, maybe, or Kratua. That monster must have existed, earlier, too, don't you think?"

"Very perspicacious, old pinniped."

"Percival! When did you return?"

"Just now. And the great baleen with me."

"Was there any reason to sing in Pacifica?" sighed Porphyry the whale, lying carefully in the shallows so he wouldn't beach. The most accomplished singers of all the tribes, whales were much inclined to melancholy.

Daniel recalled yet another verse:

> *"In Pacifica all sing the melody of pearl,*
> *the gold of understanding, all whirl*
> *In endless dance 'neath sun and wave,*
> *All hail Pacifica, cove of the brave.*

"There's your evidence for singing, Porphyry—and for dancing, and for happiness. The *'gold of understanding'*! Think of it! The phrase implies that at one time relations between Saul and Kanonah were good—even if they later turned bad. So Saul and Kanonah must have spoken a single language!"

All over the estuary, heads nodded in agreement. Ranged in front of him were Porphyry the whale, Percival the dolphin, Wenceslas the walrus, Agwah the dappled seal, Glex the red seal, Goshun the sea lion, and Popocatepetl—members of seven tribes. Daniel took courage from their approval of his vision of Pacifica. A notion from his recurring dream floated to the surface of his mind.

"Saul had thirteen sons, founded thirteen tribes," Daniel began slowly. "All of us are different, all of us have strengths and talents." He pointed at various members. "Popo can get into places that are too small for a sea lion to enter, but Glex can maneuver more easily than an otter on the great open expanses of the ocean, and Agwah can find breathing holes where we thought there were none. Percy can locate things even in the dark, but he can't hump across a beach or fight in the shallows as well as Wenceslas. We must combine all our talents to find Pacifica. The thirteen tribes must be one."

Humming and agreement greeted this simple, perfect idea. "Yes, the thirteen tribes must be one tribe to find Pacifica. And we must act quickly, or else the oceans will be destroyed—that's what all the clues and signs seem to be saying, don't they? Well, here's my plan: In six moons' time, the turtle-who-is-a-riddle will return to her island to lay her eggs. I intend to be there, and to get from her the exact location of Pacifica. And before that time, I'm going to the home coves of all the tribes to ask for members of each to come with me on our journey."

Daniel paused to let his words sink in, then posed his challenge. "Who swims with me for Pacifica?"

3

The Eyes of Saul

Next evening, as moon rose, they started northward, their destination many tens of thousands of lengths away. Daniel chose night because he wanted to avoid having the two-leggeds notice his unusual tribe, now composed of the otters Popocatepetl and Palenque as well as a dolphin, a walrus, and a baleen whale. They hugged the coastline to keep within the cooler waters that the great river fed into the sea, and to prevent the tribe from encountering any of the ooze that still befouled the areas to the south.

Popo and Palenque had difficulty swimming long distances. Even though Wenceslas offered to carry Popo as he had Uxmal, Daniel did not want the otters to feel dependent and so chose an island-hopping route. When the travelers tired, they slept on firm ground, soaking up enough of the sun's rays to warm them through increasingly chilly nights. As they journeyed north the signs of biped along the coast grew more faint.

"I wonder why the bipeds don't like to live here," Anna said to Daniel one day at dawn, as they matched strokes, flipper for flipper, at the head of the swimming formation.

"Maybe they lack the proper fur and blubber," she guessed. "Fragile creatures. Too bad for them, though, because spring in the north is far sweeter than in the southern waters."

"But their floaters go everywhere," Goshun said from his position at the extreme westward point of the formation. He nodded at one such floater, trailed by screeching birds. They all slipped a few lengths underwater to see if any fish were traveling underneath it. A school of tomcod soon appeared, protected from the sun by the floater's great bulk. The tribe would have hunted those tomcod, but Wenceslas, whose sense of smell was the most acute of any in the group, wrinkled his whiskers. The great floater above, many times the size of Porphyry, was not only trailed by screaming troops of birds but also gave off the stench of large-scale fish death; Daniel thought it must contain thousands of dead hake and sculpin.

"The bipeds concentrate everything," Anna observed. "Fish. Ooze. Caves. A couple of fish is enough of a meal for any mammal smaller than Porphyry, so why kill thousands?" Daniel could only nod assent at her logic.

At twilight the bulls, cows, and younger members of the tribe formed up to hunt. The usual method was for the tribe to separate, five lengths under the waters, where each member tried to grab any fish to be seen in dark outline against the still-lighted surface of the sea. Because they were such a large tribe, and so close to the coastline, schools of fish scattered at their approach or swam well clear. So Daniel formed pairs and groups of hunters, and all had some fun while in pursuit of a meal.

Porphyry and Percival put on a great show: First, the

whale swam slowly at the surface like a biped floater, drawing unsuspecting tomcod to travel underneath him so the dolphin, with swift thrusts of his flukes, could pick them off. Then Percy descended to the cooler, deeper waters and blew out through his blowhole and mouth a stream of clicking sounds and bubbles that forced up to Porphyry's gaping jaw the tiny motes, shrimp, and other krill on which the big whale fed. In a competing show of flipper finesse, Goshun, Wenceslas, and the red-brown seal Glex—an inseparable trio—together located a school of sculpin and began a pretty attack. When the fish scattered, the hunters all turned in separate directions and by this maneuver were able to surround and snatch a half-dozen of the oily fish.

Usually, the most aggressive individual hunters were the females who were expecting, such as Marlena and Zelda. But Anna hunted just as fiercely, even though, this cycle, she was not pregnant. "It happens sometimes as we get older," Anna told Daniel. "Nothing to do about it except to keep swimming—and mating." Daniel nipped her playfully on the shoulder.

"Isn't it exciting that Filomena is going to have a pup?" Anna asked.

"I suppose so," Daniel said, but didn't mean it. The notion of Goshun being a father, and himself a grandfather, did not lie well in his stomach. They tried another subject of conversation, his own father, Tashkent, who would be a great-grandfather, but speaking of Tashkent only brought to mind that the whitefur was not hunting as he used to. Daniel had known for some time that the old bull was fading, but a moon ago Tashkent had been able to obtain his own food. Now, after the encounter with the black ooze and the strain of long-distance traveling, Tashkent was lunging haphazardly after fish. Often as not they'd escape his jaws; then he'd have difficulty making a tight turn in the water to return to the chase.

"Here, old whistler," Daniel said as he caught a meaty tomcod and tossed it to Tashkent. The whitefur grunted and chewed it down.

Popo looked quizzically at Daniel, then at Tashkent, then back at Daniel, who drew the otter aside. "I know, he's not much of a whistler," Daniel said. "Didn't Percival tell you? Tashkent is not a proper whistler in the sense that Percy is, or, as I suspect, that you are."

Popo's ears perked up and his eyes twinkled, but he said nothing, just kept swimming gently toward a distant island landfall. "We lost our true whistler and his apprentice during the typhoon, many cycles ago," Daniel explained, and went on to tell how his own grandfather, named Goshun, had reluctantly taken the title because he was old enough to remember some of the ceremonies and the legend. When old Goshun had died and Daniel had become the leader of this new tribe, Daniel had suggested that Tashkent become the tribe's storyteller, and the whitefur had accepted the position.

"Tashkent not a true whistler," Popo agreed. "No mind-shadows."

"Mind-shadows?"

"Only seen by whistlers," Percival put in as he drifted toward them.

"Tashkent may not have the knowledge and powers that

you do," Daniel said, trying to keep anger from his voice, "but he's our oldest bull and he won't be replaced if I can prevent it."

"Perhaps he should take a central role," the dolphin said with his ever-present smile. "Swim with the little ones and leave the rear to Porphyry."

"Makes sense," Daniel agreed. So did the otter. They called Porphyry to ask him if that suited him. Silent for a moment, the whale then sighed:

> "This journey of ours will require
> More than a whistler taught in fire;
> For Pacifica, once found, will need
> Its secret mysteries to be freed."

"Ah, yes," Percival said as they approached a dark and rocky island. "Pacifica must be understood, its secrets unlocked and interpreted for the world. To do that, we will need a driftwhistler."

"Driftwhistler?" Daniel asked. He had never heard the term.

"One who knows more than can be known with the senses and the waking mind; one who can fathom the subtle twists and turns of the shadow world, and use his power for the good of all sea mammals. A driftwhistler."

"Where will we come across such a creature?" Daniel asked, incredulous.

"We cannot find him," Percival answered, "but he will find us."

For Daniel, it was not a comforting thought.

By the time the moon had reached full, then slimmed and finally shed her luminous coat, the motley tribe was swimming through floating chunks of ice. Occasionally the swimmers braved a spring snowstorm, delighting in the sight of flakes touching the waves and immediately dissolving. Days had lengthened so that a whole night passed in less than one tide; this interfered with usual patterns of sleep and waking, but no one was grumpy, for all shared the excitement of approaching the birthing ground.

Bird's Neck Island came in sight. Daniel led the tribe to the east so they would approach it from the direction that would afford the most spectacular view. Percival winked at Daniel in appreciation of the experience the sea lion was readying for Porphyry, Popocatepetl, and the others who had never before swum to this remote beach.

From a hundred lengths out into the ocean, the travelers caught their first glimpse of the brown-hued, ten-times-life-size likeness of a sea lion that topped the island. Resting majestically on a high point above the tundra and the sandy hauling ground, an image of Great Beachmaster Saul with his head and shoulders erect and flippers outstretched stared out into the ocean with multicolored eyes, challenging all intruders. Made of bone and carapace, driftwood and stones, sinew and bottom clay, with abalone shells gleaming as eyes, the statue had vastly changed the lives of the colony of dappled seals who used the island as their birthing place. Three cycles ago Daniel had created the statue, aided by seal and sea-lion bulls. For countless springs before, biped hunters had come to attack the new-born, white-coated seal pups, clubbing them to death and ripping the white coats from their bodies. When, one foggy dawn, the hunters came to kill but were stopped in their floaters by the sight of Saul protecting the island, they had not harmed the seal pups, and they never again set foot on Bird's Neck except to bring food and flowers to lay between the statue's immense flippers.

Porphyry and Popocatepetl hovered, their jaws slack, eyes fixed on the great icon. They turned slowly to find Daniel observing them from the rough surf nearer the beach, and nodded their heads in solemn approval.

The tribe's cows had no time for admiring the scenery. Sight of the birthing place had given rise to the first pangs of the process, and they hurried ashore. Many bulls had to fight for space along the hauling ground, opposed by resident bulls of the dappled seals who sought to maintain their own territory—and their harems of cows, for this was high mating season, too. Meeyon, whose home range this once had been, was surrounded by her relatives; she urged her daughter Filomena—mate to Goshun, Daniel's son—to find a spot on the beach and get comfortable, because the pup in her would soon want to come out. Actually, both mother and daughter were pregnant, and their groans quickly rose in the air. Agwah, her bull, had less of an easy time even though he had been born on this island; now of a size to be a threat to the dominant bulls, he had to fend them off to secure space for his mate and daughter on the beach. Filly was actually Goshun's responsibility, but he was busy sparring with the first seal bull on the beach; Daniel noted that the adolescent was more interested in fighting than in maneuvering to get a space for his cow. He'd have to speak to Goshun about that. No dappled seal fought Daniel; in these waters, he was a hero.

While Anna searched over the tundra grass of the low-lying island for old friends among the cousins, Daniel sought Lokat, his old mentor and the beachmaster of the dappled seals. The gray dappled seal bull was at the southern edge of the beach, locked in combat with a younger and obviously stronger bull named Kwivir, whom Daniel recognized. Though both seal bulls pushed and shoved, Lokat's shoulders and neck were bloody, while Kwivir was unmarked. With a quick maneuver, Kwivir bit Lokat's foreflipper, causing him to veer to one side, then turned him on his back. In a moment, the challenger's jaws were poised over Lokat's neck. Lokat ceased moving—a gesture of submission—and Kwivir slid off and let Lokat right himself and lurch away. The dappled seals now had a new beachmaster.

Bloody though Lokat was, he seemed about to head for the second most dominant bull, to see if he could best him; if the usual pattern were followed, Lokat would fight until he had established a new place in the order of bulls. He might hold that position for a moon-quarter, a day, or even for only a tide before another young bull would challenge it. The inevitable result for Lokat would be a series of defeats and a slow descent to a position where no one in the tribe would give him much consideration.

"No more fighting, old friend," Daniel said to him by way of greeting.

"Out of my way, sea lion," Lokat growled, violence in his eyes.

Daniel interposed his much larger body between the panting Lokat and his likely target. "The next bull may not be so inclined to let you up without removing half your flipper," Daniel said sharply. "Better to stop fighting now and accept the fact that your time is past."

"Easy for you to say, Daniel," Lokat responded, but didn't attempt to get around the sea lion, even though the second most dominant bull was trumpeting his challenge to all males on the beach. Daniel kept talking quietly, suggesting how much he himself had learned about being a proper leader from having observed Lokat. The old bull was just beginning to calm down when Daniel's attention was drawn to the beach, where his adolescent daughter Parduk was being pursued by the aggressive new beach-master of the dappled seal tribe. He seemed intent on mating. Daniel charged over the tundra toward Kwivir.

"What do you think you're doing?" Daniel bawled at the sea bull, who took one look at the fur bristling on the neck of the much larger sea lion and hopped away from Parduk. Daniel was set to give Parduk a lecture about being cautious on the hauling ground. She flopped on the beach, her face in a pout, clearly disappointed at Daniel's interference.

"And just what do you think *you're* doing?" said Anna, who came rushing over. "This is the time and place for mating."

"But, Anna, she's so young!"

"She's four cycles old. Her body is ready, Daniel."

"It's the maturity of her mind that concerns me."

"She's an adult, Daniel, whether you like it or not. So let her be one."

As usual, Anna was correct, and so Daniel shook his head and looked away from the hauling ground. On the beach, Daniel caught sight of Goshun in the process of showing off for some of the more mature dappled female seals. This was the season for the bulls to couple with as many females as possible. There was Goshun, preening for the cows, demonstrating his size and sleek muscles, conversing gaily with them. In a few moments, he'd be trying to cover and mate the seal cows. Daniel started to take pride in his son's activities, until he remembered how silly he felt at having tried to prevent his daughter from mating. Let them both be, he reminded himself, and trotted away.

~~~~~

Bird's Neck Island was mostly still, this night. The starry outline of Saul in the sky, flippers outstretched, the brightest light twinkling as his eye, had never been more vivid. On the island, most of the sea mammals slept, but the wind brought Daniel the moans of cows trying to give birth and of pups struggling to emerge into the world. Daniel felt old: His daughter was being chased by bulls. His son was mating with many partners. His first grandpup had been born. His elderly father was so enfeebled that he had to be fed. Lokat's days of dominance were gone; could Daniel's own end soon?

The sun's first glow reddened the horizon to the east. He heard the caws of sea gulls, swiveled his neck to look up at the giant statue of the great ancestor, and became alarmed. Birds hovered around its head. A dozen sea gulls pecked savagely at the abalone-shell eyes sparkling in the early rays of the sun. Daniel barked and the sea gulls scattered out to sea. But their attack had left the multicolored eyes of the statue blank!

Daniel screamed loud enough to wake Anna, dozing nearby.

"What's the matter, Daniel?"

"The sea gulls—they've blinded Saul! Don't you see what they've done to the eyes?" Daniel asked, his voice trembling.

Anna looked, and then was silent for a moment, as if embarrassed to say anything. Daniel looked again at the statue. The sun had risen more fully above the horizon now, and Saul's eyes blazed with reflected glory. "Saul's eyes look fine to me," Anna said. "Did you have a bad dream?"

"I wasn't dreaming. Sea gulls pecked at the eyes, and I chased them away, but they had blinded the statue," Daniel insisted. Anna did not reply, just settled down to get a few more moments of rest. "It was real," Daniel said again, in a lower voice. "I saw it with my eyes and I know it in my heart. It was real."

4

Learning to Whistle

Pups were being born all over the hauling ground of Bird's Neck Island. Some were the white-coated pups of the dappled seals. There were no pure sea-lion pups this cycle, but newborns included several pups of mixed parentage, such as the son of Goshun and Filomena, whom they named after their host, Lokat, who pronounced himself touched by the honor. Daniel was pleased, too. Goshun, Lokat, and Tashkent were now not only names in a single phrase of the legend, but living beings related closely by blood. His own grandfather Goshun, who had taught Daniel himself so much about the legend, would have approved this naming.

Even though the danger from hunters was no more, because of the statue that protected the island, the dappled seals clung to their old ways, refusing to name their own newborns at birth. They waited until the next moon, when the white birth coats were shed and the pups were becoming dappled like their parents. The white-coated pups were beautiful and playful enough to stir anyone's heart, and for a while Daniel pushed out of mind the spoiling of the oceans and the need to find Pacifica. He gazed wonderingly at the astonishment of the very young at encountering a wave, a shell, a passing bird. Maybe the prime purpose of the pups was to teach parents and grandparents to see the world anew. Daniel told Goshun to stop running after every available female and attend to the marvel of a first-born son. Goshun accepted this mild criticism, and for a few days the fierce young bull played with little Lokat and seemed to soften.

That the statue's fame had spread beyond the dappled seals was evident when a phalanx of elephant seals assaulted the beach to use it as a birthing ground. Their home territory was thousands of lengths to the northwest. Elephant bulls were distinguished by their long, thick, bulbous noses that to Daniel made them appear odd and menacing. However, as elephants were larger than sea lions and many times the size of other seals, they easily cleared beach space for their females and brooked no nonsense from the resident bulls, even Kwivir, the new dappled beachmaster.

Daniel recognized one of the largest of the elephant bulls from cycles ago as Nezan, whistler of the tribe and bearer of the old and honorable name mentioned in the legend. It was Nezan who had first recited to him the *"Iceberg melt and mountains fly"* verse. Nezan nodded at Daniel, too, but his path was blocked by Wenceslas the walrus—an animal just his size, whose formidable tusks were raised in an attack posture. Daniel hurried to try and defuse the confrontation, and arrived just as the gruff-voiced Nezan sidled up to Wenceslas and said, "Tell me honestly, did you ever see an animal as ugly as me?"

A low sound began in Wenceslas's throat and soon shook through his entire body until he was laughing hard enough to forget about his wish to block the elephant's path. Nezan hastily lumbered past Wenceslas toward the hauling ground. Daniel chortled as well—until Nezan headed straight for Parduk.

The next two days were agony for Daniel. He tried not to interfere while Nezan courted and mated with his daughter. "No mother or father ever thought a suitor good enough for a beautiful daughter," Anna counseled, and admitted she had doubts about the enormous elephant seal, too. Finally, they agreed that interfering would do no one any good.

Daniel stayed away from Nezan, though the elephant conversed animatedly with Popocatepetl and with one-eyed Vaz, whistler of the dappled seals. Daniel sang a verse to himself that had all of their names:

> *"Thirteen, the sons of Beachmaster Saul!*
> *Listen, lions, and name them all:*
> *Diarmuid, Zorn, and Achitopel,*
> *Hagis, Daniel, Popocatepetl,*
> *Goshun, Lokat, and Tashkent,*
> *Siwaga's tears, Porphyry's lament,*
> *Nezan's nose, the eyes of Vaz,*
> *Whatever one wants, the other has."*

It was ironic that the legend should refer to two eyes, when this particular Vaz had only one functioning eye. Was "Nezan's nose" similarly impaired?

The days grew longer and the nights shorter, until the sky was dark only long enough to offer a glimpse of the constellation of the Great Sea Lion before the sky lightened and the stars faded out. Then came that precious moment in the cycle called the white night. The sun was eaten by the sea, but the sky did not really darken. The various tribes gathered at the edge of the beach—Percival and Porphyry lolled offshore—to fast and call for the darkness that would allow Beachmaster Saul's return to the sky.

The white night ended when some member of the tribe spotted Saul's eye-star. Traditionally, if a youngster spotted this, he was then trained as a whistler's apprentice.

"There's the eye-star," Daniel yelled when he saw it. And everyone looked in the direction he pointed; sure enough, it was there.

"Well, big flippers," Popo said to Daniel. "Maybe you be whistler yet."

Daniel didn't know what to think, but contented himself with the thought of the kamarla that usually followed the end of the white night. During a kamarla, everyone nestled near to everyone else, hardly moving, bodies warm, sated with food and overlapping, drifting in and out of sleep. As this kamarla of the north began, Daniel felt his mind flowing out to touch those of the cousins near him. He was happy. His tribe was expanding in time to include a new generation, and was also broadening its boundaries. Once Daniel had shared a beach with several thousand red-brown seals; that kamarla experience had owed its power to the sheer mass of minds and bodies. This one was stronger, because the participants came from eight of the thirteen kinds of sea mammals: otter, dolphin, whale, elephant seal, dappled seal, red seal, walrus, and sea lion. He could feel the mental caresses of Popo, Percy, Porphyry, Nezan, and Vaz, their minds shooting with his along an endless curl of surf. Suddenly, Daniel realized that all these members of other tribes were whistlers. It was as clear to him as his vision of the birds pecking out the eyes of the statue.

"Did I really see that?" he asked them in his dream.

"You imagined what might happen if the statue were unprotected," Nezan answered.

As Daniel tried to understand that, a vision floated in on the endless curl of surf. It was Anna, who was a beautiful light, the color of a rose. She was saying something dark about Filomena and little Lokat. He saw them far below, on the tundra, moaning and writhing. Was he awake or asleep? This was a powerful kamarla! There was whistler Vaz rolling the mother, the pup, and himself in dust-gray lichens, making them appear white and ghostly. There was Goshun, barking at the tribe: Wenceslas to stand guard here, Glex to seek extra fish there, Porphyry to take care not to beach. There were Nezan and Popo, heading off into the waters.

To help the mother and pup Daniel plunged into the poultice of ghost-gray lichens and rolled about. Vaz, alarmed, told him he was brave to do this, but must now close his eyes to follow the sick ones into the realm in which he had seen the birds peck at the statue's eyes. He closed his eyes and found himself instantly floating beneath the surface of a shadowy sea at a depth where the sun could hardly be seen. He understood that he was on a journey with Vaz, Filomena, and little Lokat, traveling swiftly on a friendly current to ask forgiveness of the moon in her home cove. Two monsters attacked. The north wind descended toward them with hard, white tentacles that sought to encircle and crush. And the sea floor loomed up in swirls, a shape without shape, a blinding, choking wind of sand and shell.

The sand stung Daniel's left foreflipper. No blood flowed; Daniel just felt a throbbing that would not cease. He must protect his charges from these monsters without beating hearts. Swallowing seawater in huge amounts, he expelled it at the sand-being, which scattered. Then he moved his flippers at eye-dazzling speed to melt the icy tentacles of the north wind. These actions only momentarily deterred the monsters: The sands re-formed and were powerful again; the wind dripped ice to cover the scars he made in it. In moments, he, Filomena, and little Lokat would be devoured, skewered by the wind, or blasted into sand. Daniel called out for help from Vaz, who summoned others to appear and help. Popocatepetl slipped through to lead them in a channel the width of a minnow where the monsters found it hard to follow. Porphyry inhaled all the swirling sand; Esmeralda the polar bear slashed the icy wind with claws of fire. Nezan and Percival sang and laughed until the danger dissolved into particles in the water and sank toward the bottom.

Daniel wanted to surface, and thrust upward. But when he broke through, he found himself not in the ocean but on the tundra. It was day, and clouds obscuring the sun revealed that a storm had just passed. It was warm. Maybe everything was back to normal! Filomena and Lokat slept with openmouthed innocence, and Daniel knew from the look of them that they had returned to health. Just off-shore, the ever-smiling Percival finned lazily, but Daniel felt as if he could see Percy's heart beating: It was a multifaceted abalone shell, throbbing with the moving sunlight. Goshun stared down at Daniel from the rocks above the tundra; a blue shadow vibrated in the air around him. Daniel turned to find Anna settled in by his side, and saw something beautiful.

"Love flows from your shoulders like a fresh snow the color of pink roses," he murmured into her ear, but then was moved to ask her, "Why is our son's anger so ice-blue? We really must help him to warmth."

Anna looked at him fearfully. "Are you all right now, Daniel?"

"I am fine, and so are they," he responded, indicating Filomena and little Lokat. "The sand- and wind-monsters could not devour us."

"Yes, there was a great storm," Anna nodded, stroking his flipper.

"The whistlers helped me fight them."

Anna took a deep breath, keeping her head down and her eyes open. "Daniel," she said slowly, "you're becoming so different that it's scary."

After a while, the rose-colored drape flowing from Anna's shoulders went away, as did the blue shimmer that surrounded Goshun, and the beating of Percival's multicolored heart—but Daniel knew that his understanding of these truths about his family and friends would not go away.

～～～

Two days later, a high howl drifted to Daniel from the direction of the continent. Esmeralda! A commotion offshore soon revealed the approach of Popocatepetl, Palenque, and the swimming white bear. It was quite something to see the great white polar bear and the small otters, for their swimming shapes were very similar though their sizes differed.

"I saw you the other night, Esme," Daniel said. "Didn't I?"

The white polar bear would not answer that question, but did say, "I told you one day we would hunt together."

Another whistler, Daniel concluded, and figured out that she had come for something more than the naming ceremony for the dappled seals. Then Nezan arrived with Parduk. He could see by the light in his daughter's eyes that they were firmly mated—you didn't need to be a whistler to tell that! But he understood, now, why these creatures from the other tribes had come to this spot.

A few days later, as the dappled seals readied themselves to start back to their home cove, directly east on the coast of the continent, Daniel announced that he and the whistlers were going to stay for a moon or so on Bird's Neck while the remainder of his tribe would go with the dappled cousins to enjoy the lovely summer in their home cove.

"We'll be fine," Anna said to Daniel as they nuzzled in the surf. She reached forward with a hind flipper to scratch near her ear. "There won't be any problems. Goshun can lead us."

"Goshun's not ready to lead the tribe," Daniel bristled. "A beachmaster has to be more than big; he has to make others want to follow him."

"Wenceslas and Glex follow Goshun all the time."

"Born followers! Goshun has no experience and lacks judgment."

"How can he get experience without some time as an actual leader?"

Daniel was not entirely convinced, but eventually agreed to let the tribe go to the inlet without him. They took to the water smartly, and as they reached the surf point, Goshun shouted, "Wenceslas, take up the rear!" The walrus slipped back through the formation to the guard position, and Daniel grudgingly had to admit that were he leading the group, he too would have placed Wenceslas there.

Daniel watched the swimming seals, sea lions, Palenque, and Wenceslas disappear toward the continent. On the beach and in the waters near the giant statue of Beach-master Saul were the only sea mammals left on Bird's Neck: the whistlers Vaz, Nezan, Percival, Porphyry, Esmeralda, Lokat, and Popocatepetl. A powerful lot! Daniel sighed and trotted toward them. It was time for his whistling lessons to begin.

~~~~~~

They had gathered, they told him, because he had qualities they wished to see in a driftwhistler. None knew what a driftwhistler would be, but Daniel had demonstrated traits that were unusual. Repeatedly, and over several cycles, he had shown his concern for all sea mammals, by doing everything from making the statue to protecting the southern archipelago from the red tide and, just recently, by his willingness to enter into the dangerous realm of the spirit to assist in the rescue of Filomena and little Lokat.

His eagerness to follow the clues of the legend, his dream of thirteen tribes uniting to prevent the destruction of the oceans, even the vision of the birds pecking out the eyes of Saul—all these suggested that he was a sea mammal of great promise.

To his astonishment, Daniel learned that Percival had seen his qualities cycles ago, and had forsaken his own tribe in order to assist Daniel in his development.

"And I believed you really thought all the time that I was dumb!"

"Not dumb, Daniel, just terminally stubborn," Percival grinned.

There were more revelations for Daniel. He learned that his first testing had been in the sargasso, when four whistlers and he had faced down the one-horned, nameless beast.

"Four whistlers! Lavender the killer whale is a whistler as well?" They nodded. "Then we'll have to find her if we're going to Pacifica."

Popocatepetl piped up, "Lots to learn first, old flipper."

His escape from the north wind and the sea floor, they warned him, had been that of a fortunate novice. He had sensed enough to call for help from the whistlers near him; without it, he might not have emerged alive. To truly make use of all the power of the oceans he must study the craft of whistlerdom.

For the next moon, Daniel received instruction. Every animal, and every plant, had both obvious characteristics and those that could be understood only through deep study of what was not easily or usually seen—auras such as those Daniel had temporarily sensed after the kamarla, links between creatures in the seas and those in the sky, such as that of the old turtle and the moon. From Lokat he learned about poultices and potions to heal the sick; from Popocatepetl and Esmeralda, verses to whisper when attempting to be invisible to all pursuers; from Percival and Porphyry, ways to pay heed and feel with his whiskers what the sea might tell him about approaching friends and foes. This type of moss was good for stomach upset; that sort of butterfly could be crushed and applied to relieve the pain inflicted by nettles.

Daniel believed he was entering into his study fully but was only occasionally successful: Some auras he saw, more he missed. Moreover, his herbal potions stank and his lichen poultices were often ineffective. He was seldom able to understand much about the coming weather, or to figure out how certain creatures in the sea would behave. Missing Anna and the pups, and feeling inadequate to his new endeavors, he often sat with his nostrils alert for breezes coming from the inlet shore, many lengths to the east, wondering how his tribe and his love were getting along without him.

One day in midsummer Esmeralda asked him to swim close to the stinging tentacles of a jellyfish but not to let them harm him. The way to do it was to convince the jellyfish not to think of him as either food or danger.

"You must approach with your mind clear of fear, and focused only upon the task," Esmeralda advised. Daniel prepared himself by doing deep dives until his muscles were tired, then swam closer to this floating jellyfish than he had ever done to any other without getting stung—but it was not enough; he brushed by one tentacle and it let loose its poison, burning his left hind flipper. A whole tide went by before feeling returning to the limb.

Esmeralda took him aside and confided: "In order to achieve mastery of the whistler's world, Daniel, you must give up your mastery of the everyday world."

"I don't understand. What do you mean?"

"You must give up being beachmaster of the tribe."

Daniel shook his head. "That," he said, "I shall never willingly do."

~~~~~

It was late summer when Daniel and the whistlers crossed to the coastal inlet. The cove served as the dappled seal colony's home except during the rutting and birthing season. Anna, on a high rock watching the ocean for their arrival, hopped eagerly to greet him. "I felt you'd be coming back today," she said. Daniel had tried very hard to send his mate just this message mentally, and was pleased at the results. They embraced and spent some time lying side by side in the morning sun. Goshun was enjoying the leadership of the tribe. The adolescent kept a sharp eye out for the best sleeping perches, covered many of the females when he felt like it, and demanded respect from all. When he sauntered over to Daniel he did not immediately bend his neck to the beachmaster.

"So," Daniel said to Goshun, "you want this awful job?"

"I can handle it, Daniel," Goshun responded. "I've proved that."

"Being in charge when there's no danger is a pleasure, son, but that's not all there is to it. You'll lead your own tribe in due time."

"I'm stronger than you are," Goshun bristled, the fur on his nape beginning to rise up. Daniel looked to the whistlers who had been his tutors on Bird's Neck. They had asked him to give up his leadership in order to better enter the spirit world, but he had refused. Now Goshun wanted to fight for that leadership. With Daniel's new knowledge, it would be simple for him to best Goshun— a bit of an illusion, or strange sounds that might distract or alarm the bull—but Esmeralda shook her head slightly. Daniel understood that she was telling him that if he felt he must keep the beachmastership now, he must do so without resort to a whistler's powers. He nodded to the big bear.

He decided to investigate the progress of his grand-pup, little Lokat, and the other newborns. When Goshun pursued him, snapping at his flippers, trying to irritate him into fighting, Daniel determinedly went about the business of greeting his old followers and inquiring about their new offspring. As he had hoped, in doing so he re-established bonds, and soon Agwah, Meeyon, and the others no longer looked up every so often for direction from Goshun. The younger bull was annoyed, but could not alter the dominance order so long as Daniel chose not to give way.

Daniel had won, but nonetheless felt downhearted.

His time in isolation had not been completely successful. Without mastery in the techniques of navigating in the whistler's domain, how would he ever find Pacifica, much less fathom its secrets? Maybe along the path to Pacifica he would somehow learn what was necessary to act as a driftwhistler.

In support of that notion, Popo suggested that the tribe leave as soon as possible for the southern archipelago. The otter believed some problems among his own kind required assistance. Also, he reported that Palenque had spotted bipeds observing the motley pinniped tribe in the inlet while the whistlers had been on Bird's Neck—not the hunter bipeds, but other two-leggeds whose skin was lighter and who held glass devices to their eyes.

Their leave-taking of the dappled seals was casual, as if nothing depended on it. After a last sunset ceremony, Daniel and his comrades bade brief farewells and set out down the coastline, traveling at modest speed in the water. They were of nine of the thirteen lines descended from Saul—Esmeralda the polar bear; the otters Popocatepetl and Palenque; Nezan the elephant seal; dappled seals Mee-yon, Agwah, Filomena, and several others of old Lokat's line; Glex the red seal; Wenceslas the walrus; the dolphin Percival; the whale Porphyry; and many sea lions, including Daniel, Anna, her sisters Marlena and Zelda, and their pups. "This is a gathering such as has not been seen in many thousands of moons, if ever there was a similar group assembled," Percival confided as they swam the lead positions.

Daniel nodded, and resisted the urge to tell the dolphin that he hadn't seen anything yet. In his mind, the idea of a thirteen-tribe group was becoming more real with each passing tide. Daniel recounted noses: nine of the thirteen tribes who were descended from Saul. He knew of a killer whale, a narwhal, and a manatee. That would make twelve, if all could be found. But what about the thirteenth tribe, who, legend had it, had disappeared?

"Ah, yes," Percival said with his toothy grin, "the regrettably lost ones. Or is it we who are lost because we have not found them?"

"Must you be so exasperating, Percy?"

"Only when necessary."

As they traveled south, down the coastline of the continent, no sharks attacked. There were no storms that could not be easily weathered. And, although evidence of biped habitation grew more apparent as they proceeded southward along the coast—the floating white kelplike stuff, the brown slime pouring from metal tube worms at the continent's edge that emptied into the ocean—it was, all things considered, a quiet journey. To accommodate the pace of the pups and old Tashkent, the travelers did not make as much progress each day as Daniel would have liked. These stragglers had difficulty swimming for more than a quarter-tide without rest. How curious it was that near the end of life an animal was nearly as helpless as at the beginning! But though Tashkent's mind wandered and he was often unable to obtain his own food, he struggled lionfully onward.

In a shallow, floating kelp bed just north of the estuary, the travelers found the entire colony of otters chasing crustaceans among the enormous leaves. Daniel's motley tribe eagerly nibbled at the kelp; the greenery was a wonderful variation on their usual diet of fish, clams, and squid. Percival winked at Daniel, his mouth full of leaves; it had been in a kelp bed that they had first met. Daniel grinned, recalling their initial butting fight—so long ago, and yet it felt as if it were only a quarter-moon past. If the visitors were having fun, Popo, usually so happy and mischievous, appeared grave.

"This used to be playbed. But now must be more, because bathing hole is algae and silt," Popo said.

Palenque lamented, "No more sweet baths, no more mud palaces, no more nice reeds."

"Colony moved to kelp bed forever," Popo explained in his squeaky voice. "Never again sleep on big shore. Islands or boulders only."

It was uncomfortable not being able to touch hard ground once in a while, and annoying to go without a favorite food. But the otters had now been deprived of an even greater part of their lives—fresh water: The small swimmers had used sweet water to bathe off excess salt that remained in their fur. How would they get rid of it if all the sweet-water holes had become befouled? Just the thought of being unable to rid himself of an irritant made Daniel's own skin itchy. With his hind flippers he scratched around his ears, and noticed many of his comrades doing the same. He offered to have all the otters come on the quest for Pacifica. Popo said no. Sooner or later, the otter reasoned, they'd have to adjust to a life without fresh water or safe ground to sleep on, and they might as well do it now. Daniel countered that they might find a better estuary, but no otter wanted to leave the area where generations of ancestors had lived, fished, and gone to sand.

What Daniel could not figure out was another metal shelf full of bipeds on the point of the coast near the kelp bed; in it, he glimpsed the sun reflecting off biped glasses. The bipeds seemed to have moved their watching-shelf from the estuary to the kelp bed. If they were concerned for the otters, why not stop fellow bipeds from spoiling the otter's range in the estuary?

As they coursed southward along the coast the weather grew warmer and there were more and more signs of biped habitation. A quarter-moon after leaving the kelp bed, the tribe was within easy trawling distance of Daniel's old home cove. It had been in that small, near-perfect place of gentle waves, mild climate, and ample perches that Daniel, Anna, Marlena, and Zelda had grown up, under the leadership of Tashkent. Of course, Tashkent had not truly been in charge there, for all his heavy-flippered roaring: Food, shelter, warmth, and daily routines in the cove had been supplied and controlled by bipeds. The sea lions had lived in captivity, though no physical barrier had kept them from the open sea. From this too-pleasant trap Daniel alone had first escaped. Later, he had returned to woo Anna, and even made a third trip after Goshun was born. That was when he had convinced Tashkent as well as Anna's birth-cohort sisters to join his new tribe.

In the next moons he had swum wide of the cove, not wishing to have anything to do with the place. Now, however, as they journeyed down the coast, Porphyry, Percival, and Popo said they could feel vibrations of distress coming from that area. Daniel tried hard to be sensitive to these, and eventually felt them as well. He then announced that the tribe would have to pay a visit to the old home cove.

They reached the vicinity of Small Crab Island, the jumping-off place for an approach to the cove. Here, too, was a spit of land filled with memories: of his own time of testing, of his first pleasure-time with Anna, of the moment when he had proclaimed to his extended family that they would henceforth roam the seas in search of Pacifica. Now a powerful tribe rested on the small rocks, looking east to a cove that seemed so inviting, so caressing, with its encircling arms and narrow entryway and mountain background. After warning the new members that the cove was considerably more dangerous than it appeared, Daniel asked all to submerge and headed eastward. The tribe's diversity would attract attention—and attention from bipeds never brought sea mammals anything good.

As they neared the opening, Daniel was flabbergasted to see, stretched between the two arms of rock, a submerged metal barrier connecting the arms from a point ten lengths above the surface all the way down to the sandy bottom. No sea mammal could get into or out of the cove through this. The metal barrier was thin, but as Popo soon found out, it bit back like an electric eel. Daniel nodded the tribe to the outer rim, where they conferred. "This isn't good," Daniel whispered, "but I can climb in over the rocks without getting shocked. The rest of you stay out here—or go to Small Crab Island and wait for me."

"No needless heroics," Percival advised. "The quest requires your presence intact."

"I'll be a good pup," Daniel grinned. "I'm just going to take a look."

"I'm coming with you," Anna piped up. "It was my home, too, Daniel." She looked as if she might give way to anger if he objected.

"A pair will be less obvious than just one of us?"

"That's right."

Again, Daniel had to agree. Together, they headed toward the cove.

5

Lavender's Break

*A*nna and Daniel made a cautious approach over the rocks of the southern arm, hugging the ground and stopping at Bright Corner, the high tide pool that overlooked the Singing Stones and the entire breadth of the cove. As they neared the inside of the cove, biped music assaulted their ears. Flat on the tide pool, they tried to be inconspicuous. Not only did a barrier lay across the entrance to the cove, but also the entire character of their old home place had been altered. Multicolored kelp strands and airtoys dotted the upper ridges. Toward the waterline, what had once been natural perches had been pounded by the bipeds into tiers of stone steps too narrow to accommodate reclining pinnipeds, though bipeds could sit on them. In the past, watchers had ranged only along the upper part of the cove arms, peering occasionally at sea-mammal swimmers and perch-sitters. Now, bipeds on the stone seats were able to get closer to the sea lions than ever before; and more glass-fronted caves inside the arms, below the surface of the water, allowed greater numbers of bipeds to peek at the colony.

The cove's alterations paled in contrast to the changes

in the resident sea lions. None were young, since no pups had been born in the cove in many a cycle. Esther and Blossom were Tashkent's age, and the remaining dozen or so, though younger than that, seemed as fat and sluggish, their gaze continually fixed at the bipeds on the upper perches, expecting food or awaiting commands. Daniel's birth brothers Hagis and Achitopel, co-beachmasters of the cove, were prime examples. A long, flat piece of wood had been extended out from the perch above Elbow Overhang; as Anna and Daniel watched, Hagis, now nearly as blubbery as Wenceslas, wobbled out onto the edge of the wood. Down below, in the calm waves, Achitopel waved a flipper to encourage him to come on down. The music boomed. On the wooden perch, Hagis raised his body on his foreflippers so that his hindquarters were in the air, and then flipped over backward and dove into the cove with an inelegant splash. The bipeds on the seats clapped their hands, showed their teeth, and made bird noises. Then the sea lions scattered around the cove made the same gestures, slapping foreflippers together or hitting them against their flanks, barking nonsensically for the delight of the bipeds. Hagis and Achitopel leaped out onto a special perch, where a biped trainer fed them a fish apiece. Daniel and Anna were stunned by their old brothers' behavior.

More surprises followed. In the water a floating perch had been placed. Old Esther and Blossom climbed on it and clamped their teeth over some strange-looking devices that made blaring noises; they set up a rhythmic bleat that served as background for Larnach and Gwillyn, two slightly younger cows, to toss airtoys back and forth, balancing them on their noses. Meanwhile, the trainer affixed various pieces of biped coverings to Hagis and Achitopel— a head covering for the former, a brightly colored frond around the midsection for the latter. In a culminating movement, as the old cows sounded blaring noises and the middle-aged ones nosed airtoys about, Hagis and Achitopel chased each other around the land perches, each holding a piece of wood in his mouth; when one struck the other, the second jumped in the air and barked. The whole display provoked many bipedian handclaps and birdcalls.

The music slowed and calmed. Esther, Blossom, and the others headed for the perches on the southern arm, where they were rewarded with fish, and with something else that Anna recognized. "Wafers," Anna said to Daniel. "And it's not even near feeding time."

"Or time for the ceremoney of the dying sun—but they probably don't honor the sun any longer." Just when they thought the worst must be over, all the sea lions and the watching bipeds turned to gaze at a spot in the northern cove arm. Biped markings hung above it. Part of the cove wall slid back at just that point—Daniel hadn't known it was possible to make an opening in these rocks—and out swam a black-and-white female killer whale, five times the size of a sea-lion bull. "Lavender," sighed Daniel. "Now the distress signals make sense."

"I can't believe it," Anna whispered to Daniel. "Killer whales *eat* sea lions. Don't the bipeds know that? Look how afraid Larnach is!"

"Well, they don't eat sea lions all the time, only when there's no other food. And besides, Lavender wouldn't harm any relative of mine." Daniel explained to Anna that he had met Lavender on the adventure in the sargasso, the one he had shared with Percival, Popo, and Esmeralda.

"Lavender's a whistler, too, I suppose," Anna said drily; she wasn't entirely pleased by animals whose minds floated here and there. "If she's so powerful, what's she doing in here?" One answer came immediately. Lavender raced around the cove, then leaped high in the air, flipped over, and went back in—splashing water onto perches on which some bipeds sat. They shrieked with alarm, then, realizing that it was only water, showed their teeth and clapped their hands. So: Lavender, too, was a performer. But the cove's wide-eyed sea lions cowered against the stones, their ancient fear of the killer whale unabated. A biped trainer climbed atop the long wooden perch from which Hagis had earlier somersaulted, and held a fish by its tail. Lavender leaped to get it. The snap of her jaws as she grabbed the fish sent shivers down both Anna's and Daniel's spines.

"Pretty good leap, wasn't it, Daniel?" Lavender squealed on her graceful descent to the waters. "We'll chat when I'm finished working."

"She recognizes you," Anna said, nudging him with her foreflipper.

Open-mouthed, Daniel nodded. In the next awful moments, Lavender allowed one biped to ride her back, chased a terrified Larnach around the cove, and did a spectacular leap to nuzzle noses with the biped female who stood on the high perch. After that, all the cove's sea lions raced madly ahead of her while the music blossomed and the watching bipeds clapped. Eventually Lavender chased all the sea lions to their perches—where they received still more fish and wafers—and swam alone in the bay, doing great lazy circles about the perimeter. Only when the music ceased did the watching bipeds get up and walk toward the cliff at the back of the cove.

~~~~~~~

That evening, on the rocks of Small Crab Island, Daniel and the tribe watched the sea swallow the sun and sang of the approach of night. Daniel had wanted to celebrate at the Singing Stones of his youth, but the events of the day seemed to emphasize the lesson of the old sea-lion saying: You cannot swim in the same waters twice. Knowing that his home had been altered beyond recognition, and that from now on the good old days would exist only in memory, gave Daniel strength: There was nowhere to go but onward, to seek Pacifica and make a new future. The nearness of the home cove seemed to reinvigorate Tashkent, Daniel's old father, whose mind had wandered greatly of late. The whitefur felt badly about the changes Daniel reported. After all, he said with feeling, it had been under his own beachmastership that the tribe had begun the long slide into the captivity that was now the lot of the cove's remaining sea lions.

"Yes, old father—but you had little choice, back then. The typhoon had sent so many to sand, and the rest would have gone if you'd continued to swim the open ocean with only a few tribal members."

"True, true. But my decision to go with the bipeds turned out badly."

"That was long ago," Daniel interrupted. "Don't think

about it. Lavender told me she sensed the presence of many whistlers nearby, and knew they would help her. I promised to rescue her."

"What about the sea lions in the cove?" Marlena asked. "Did any of them want to be rescued? Any of the cows?"

"Not really," Anna observed. "Old Esther didn't say no outright, but all the others told me that living there wasn't so bad, and who knew what dangers might lurk outside! Can you believe that? They've been telling the same old tales since I was a pup!"

"Old Esther," Tashkent mused. "She was stunning in her youth."

"Well, Daniel," Percival said, "what ought we to do?"

"Don't any of you whistlers have a plan?" Daniel wondered, feigning innocence. "After all, you're so much smarter and more learned than I am."

"In some matters, perhaps, but not in dealing with complicated rescues. You're the hero, you know," Esmeralda insisted. No whistler's lichens or swift moves could make the barrier at the cave's entrance disappear.

As the whistlers suspected, Daniel did have a plan, one that involved the talents of Percival, Porphyry, Nezan, Esmeralda, and Wenceslas, the five largest members of the tribe, who would go with him to the cove. Most agreed with the idea of freeing Lavender, but there were a few objections. Killer whales were feared by many pinnipeds for their occasional hunting of seals and sea lions.

"Lavender is an old friend who'd never harm any sea lion from my tribe," Daniel insisted. "Besides, she's a whistler, and above all a cousin who will join us as a representative of the tenth tribe of the sons of Saul. We'll need cousins from all thirteen lines to make a proper approach to Pacifica."

Despite Daniel's logic, there were still some grumblers until Tashkent sat back on his haunches, reared his massive head, and spoke. "Be happy there is danger in the mission," the old bull said. "If you're not in fear of losing everything, you'll gain nothing. Only a fool refuses to consider the possibility of defeat, but only a coward fears to try the unknown." This quieted the last few objections.

As there was not a moment to lose, the five bulky bulls and Esmeralda immediately started for the cove. Goshun wanted to go as well, but Daniel said that the safety of the rest of the tribe would rest upon him, and he stayed back. It was at least a tacit admission on Daniel's part that the adolescent had led the tribe well enough during Daniel's previous absence. But Tashkent slid into the water after his big companions. "I'm going, too," the old one said.

This was the one mission for which Daniel could not tell the whitefur that he was too old or weak. Daniel bowed his head and pushed on. Now they were seven warrior swimmers.

～～～～

Under a shiny half-moon the assault team approached the metallic gates. Looking up, they saw only a few bipeds walk up and back between the Singing Stones and the cliff of the shoreline. Lavender glided about the bay while the resident sea lions lay silent on the lower perches.

To Percival and Porphyry, who could not maneuver on

land, Daniel gave the task of broaching the metal barrier with stones and driftwood. It was astounding to see the ease with which the baleen whale could lift a large boulder in his jaws, and the speed that Percival would attain while swimming with a protruding branch held between his teeth. As the dolphin and whale prepared to batter the gate, Daniel and Wenceslas hauled out over the rocks—it was simpler for the sea lion than for the walrus, who had to use his tusks to pull himself along—and then slipped into the waters of the bay to alert Lavender and any sea lions who wished to escape. Esmeralda, whose white coat might be conspicuous inside the cove, climbed up near the Singing Stones. From there she'd throw stones at the metal barrier. Nezan and Tashkent, strong but less able to ma- neuver on land, laboriously followed Daniel's lead to the crests of the southern and northern arms, there to await their moments under the moon. When Tashkent saw what had become of the old home cove, he shook his burly head in disgust, then grimly set his jaw and got ready to take part in the action to come.

Daniel and Wenceslas moved so carefully and blended in so well with the other cove inhabitants that the biped guards took no notice of them. Lavender was overjoyed to see Daniel, and readied herself for a swift run at the gates. Daniel approached the sleeping sea lions, looking for anyone who wished to *travel far in mystery.* Hagis and Achitopel ignored him; Larnach and Gwillyn weren't interested in going anywhere that the killer whale was going; and old Blossom turned up her nose, even when Daniel told her there was a two-cycle cow in the outside tribe who was named for her.

"You mean there are pups?" Esther asked. She slept next to Blossom.

"Several, including a few very small ones," Daniel nodded. "But we don't have any great-grandmothers."

Hearing this, the old cow pronounced herself ready to go. She shuddered a bit at being so near Lavender, but let herself be led out by Wenceslas along the ledges and perches of the southern arm. Once they had started their climb, Daniel signaled Esme to begin the assault.

Though she was suffering from the heat this far south, the white polar bear reared up in the full glare of the moon and threw a sharply pointed stone at a point in the barrier that seemed bent. Sparks flew from the barrier, and a ringing noise sounded. Percival ran at that point in the gate with the branch in his mouth. Just before the wood hit the barrier, Porphyry slung a broad, heavy boulder at the same spot. First the stone softened up the metal, then the wood breached it. The cracked barrier sagged and sank until it was only three or four lengths above the surface of the waves at the point of the attack.

Now that silence no longer mattered, Daniel shouted, "Hit it again! Make it low enough so Lavender can vault over."

Bipeds started to run along both walls toward the barrier. They were met by the roar and the red-nasal-sac display of Nezan the elephant seal, by the jaws and claws of Esmeralda the white polar bear—fearsome sights—as well as by Tashkent the Terrible, whose full-throated cry of anger and vengeance thrilled Daniel. The bipeds backed away, as Daniel had hoped they would, giving the dolphin and the whale more time to make further thrusts at the metal barrier, which continued to spew out spark-showers. The metal sagged further at each battering. Two or three more blows would lower it within Lavender's vaulting range. The killer whale sped quickly about the perimeter of the bay, building speed for the big jump. Wenceslas and Esther reached the crest of the southern arm, then slid and tumbled down toward the outer waters and safety.

Esmeralda and Tashkent were just about to follow them when one biped threw a net over the great white polar bear, entangling her. In her own home cove she would have brushed them aside, but here Esme was exhausted from the heat, and wasn't so strong. Two more bipeds rushed forward, intent on twisting kelp lines about her. Daniel, in the midst of climbing the north arm after Nezan, was too far away to do anything to help his tutor in whistlerdom—but Tashkent was right next to her. With a scream, the old bull began to battle. Displaying the vigor and energy of an aroused and massive sea mammal, Tashkent charged for the legs of the bipeds, swiping them with his burly shoulders and snapping at them with teeth bared. In this manner he upended and tumbled one biped, who fell into the bay with an awkward splash. The resident sea lions of the cove applauded this diving biped with flipper slaps, Daniel saw, but he could afford only a moment's chuckle because Tashkent was still in trouble. As Esme clawed her way out of the net and leaped for the waters outside the cove, the second and third bipeds turned on Tashkent, thrusting metallic sticks at him that seemed to emit the same kind of sparks coming from the slowly sinking metal barrier. Struck on a flipper, Tashkent retreated.

"Come on, Daniel," the big-nosed Nezan urged as they

began to descend to the open sea side of the northern arm. "You can't help him from here."

Daniel knew that the elephant seal was correct, but didn't like feeling unable to do anything for Tashkent, who, he now realized, was not simply retreating haphazardly from the spark-stick. "He's doing it deliberately," Daniel whispered. Tashkent was leading the bipeds out onto the wooden ledge above Elbow Overhang.

In midcove, Lavender sang, "Here goes," and then dove to the bottom, only to reappear in a rush, break the surface, and sail, tail flukes and all, no more than a mussel's breadth above the sparking metal barrier into the open waters outside the cove. Lavender was free! A cheer went up from Esther, as well as from the members of the assault team. Curiously also, there were happy noises and handclaps from some bipeds watching on the cove's arms, though not from those busy pursuing Tashkent and Esme.

"Let's make waves, big one," Lavender purred as she trolled near Porphyry. The whale cast a large, wary eye at her and silently led her out toward Small Crab.

On the rocks, Daniel hardly had time to feel elation. Esme was still struggling out of the net, while his old father edged out high above Elbow Overhang followed by two bipeds with a spark-stick who seemed to have forgotten the polar bear in their pursuit of Tashkent. Esme broke completely out of the net and scrambled for the far rim of the southern arm. As she did so, an awful roar and scream came from Tashkent. The big bull crumbled as if hit by a blow. But the spark-stick had not struck him.

"His heart," Nezan whispered. 'It's given out."

Daniel started toward his old father with an unthinking lurch—and slammed into the metal barrier with his left foreflipper. Sparks shot up, and he felt a searing pain. It was all Nezan could do to pull him off the barrier and outside of the cove. Though he was in pain, Daniel could not stop gazing at his sire. On the absurd extended wooden ledge, Tashkent tottered, then slowly toppled off and fell with a sickening flat splash into the waters and completely beneath the surface. A moment later, Tashkent's body rose slowly and simply floated on the waves. The old bull no longer moved of his own accord. Tashkent was dead.

"Come on, Daniel," Nezan urged. "He's beyond help now. You're hurt, and we must get away." Transfixed as he watched Tashkent's body wash toward the Overhang, the beachmaster could hardly move. His foreflipper was numb. Nezan had to shoulder him out into the currents of the open sea to complete their escape from the old home cove.

~~~~~

On and near Small Crab, waiting for the first rays of the sun, the tribe rested. Daniel could not shake his sadness about his father's death.

"He spoke kindly of you in the last tides," Daniel told Esther, the old grandmother cow, in the moments when she was not busily peering at the smallest of the sleeping pups. "Tashkent died so you could escape," Daniel told Lavender, the killer whale.

"It was a good death, then," Lavender said. "In full time. One cannot ask for more."

"Yes, Daniel," Anna chimed in. "You have to admit that his end was fitting: He died protecting the future of his tribe."

"That's true," said the beachmaster. "But he won't have a proper float to the sun." In the legend of Saul, when a beachmaster died, his body was decorated with stones and floated to the sun, which consumed him. However, Tashkent's body remained in the cove, and the bipeds would dispose of it in some less correct way. They wouldn't even afford it the dignity of being eaten and becoming part of another sea creature's flesh.

"The cove was Tashkent's destiny," Percival the dolphin opined. "He once made the decision to go there, made another one to leave it at the proper moment, and went back willingly, knowing full well it might be his death. In dying there he perpetuated more than his tribe—he embraced the entire range of sea mammals."

"Yes," Daniel said, feeling calmer though no less sad. "I can see that."

Daniel could also sense healing thoughts from Popo, Esme, Percy, and Lavender. He considered the shape of his father's life, how Tashkent had actually been more content in his old age than in his tempestuous youth. Everyone in the tribe was quiet for a half-tide, waiting for the sun to appear from behind the mountain over the cove, the signal for the start of the day. Now they were ten of the thirteen lines of descendants of Saul, a tribe composed of many powerful, battle-tested individuals, Daniel thought. They would see to it that Tashkent had not given up his essence in vain.

Goshun hauled next to Daniel and started to whisper something to him.

"What is it, Goshun? Speak up," Daniel said curtly.

"Well, I think that—I mean—now that Tashkent is gone, we—I mean, the sea lions—we have no whistler; and you've been learning about that, and you could do it while I—while I sort of steer the tribe."

"You want me to give up the beachmastership and become the whistler? When the tribe has so many whistlers that even the bipeds tremble?"

"It was just a suggestion."

"Not yet, my son. Not yet!"

A quarter-tide later, as the first rays of the sun glimmered beyond the mountain that loomed over the cove, the tribe set out for the southern archipelago and the birthing grounds of moon's turtle.

6

The Turtle's Silence

*F*or two moons, the motley tribe of Daniel au Fond swam south. Behind them the shores of the northern continent dwindled to the size of a floating stick and then dissolved in haze as the swimmers entered the waters of the southern archipelago, skirting the second great landmass to veer toward clusters of isolated islands. They circled Two-Tusk Isle, once home to Wenceslas, and paused at Backbone, where Glex was born.

Unlike the regions of the northern seas, these southern ones displayed mixed temperatures, here welling with cool springs, there calm with torpid heat. The travelers endured storms of grand scope, followed by sun-bleached days and clear nights on which the thirteen stars of the constellation of Saul seemed close enough to touch. The tribe crowded the air with praises for Saul, and each evening searched the horizon's luminous clouds for hints of the weather; glistening dark skies told them only that the journey must continue. Daniel had hoped that further away from the more dense areas of biped population, the seas would be unsoiled, but they were everywhere marred by bits of floating white trash, slicks of black ooze, gristlelike stuff that would not tear, and blue-green algae. The injury to Daniel's left foreflipper healed over, but feeling did not return, and his timing was off. On land, he limped; in the sea, he yawed to the left and often had to adjust course. Since he was the formation leader, his mistakes were compounded. Nonetheless, the tribe made good progress.

Pups who could hardly swim a thousand lengths a day at the start went that far in a single tide by the dark of the first moon. Old enemies such as the polar bear and the dappled seals matched rhythmic thrusts and listened to one another's heartbeats. Hunting teams became remarkably coordinated and self-effacing, the better hunters yielding some of their catch to the less proficient. No one asked where Lavender had gone when she occasionally sped off out of sight and returned sated; but several concerned themselves with spotting likely upwellings of cool water that were full of krill on which Porphyry could feed. He strained krill from the cool waters through his great mouth.

Since Daniel and his band had last been in this archipelago, a full cycle had nearly been completed. The manatee Cendrillon had pledged to meet them there this very moon, but as Daniel approached the shores of Cracked Egg, she was nowhere to be seen. Scouting parties that went into the canyon of the crack and around the molded boulder outcroppings of the small island found no trace of her. Anna was more distressed than Daniel, for she had become fond of the old tale-spinner who claimed to have known Saul and Kanonah when both were alive. "She's survived too many cycles and become too wily to have been eaten," Daniel reassured Anna. "She's probably just on a jaunt, chewing kelp. Or talking someone's ear off."

Four islands in this area made up a cluster. Cracked Egg was the outermost. To the southwest were three, closer together, that had the shapes of a double crescent, a snake, and a turtle. The recognition that these four shapes matched a pattern on the back of the great-shelled old turtle had thrilled Daniel by demonstrating that the legend was no mere story but a guide to things to come. That the birthing cove of "moon's turtle" was on the island shaped like a turtle was further evidence of the power of the legend—and it was to this westernmost island that the tribe now swam.

They approached a bay between two lava outcroppings. It formed what they thought of as the gap between the turtle's head and one of its forelimbs. Daniel was assaulted by difficult memories: the dying Sigmund, his orangutan friend, crushed against a tree by the tidal wave that thundered into the island; the farewell hand signal from his old trainer Fred, the only biped in the world who had ever treated him properly; the happy shock of learning that the blood-throated frigate bird Magellan could speak a few words of their language; the terror of learning that other bipeds were taking Goshun away on an airfloater; finally, the later joy at his son's return. Becoming older evidently meant that the world—and one's mind—filled up with memories that jostled for space with the sensations of the present. Yes, Silent Turtle Island spoke loudly.

Reaching the surf point at the outer edge of the bay between head and limb, Daniel could see that the island's former glory was changed. There were still lava and rocks at sea level, greenery beyond, and a high, volcanic peak far above, but up in the clouds the mountain seemed drab and brown, and the jungle on its slopes was touched with gray rot. When the great wave had pummeled the island it had destroyed the biped settlement next to the bay and washed away the beach on which the giant turtles had always laid their eggs. Some debris from the bipeds still remained—odd pieces of wood strewn about the rocks, twisted metal and shards of glass visible on the sandy bottom through the clear waters of the bay. There was no trace of Fred, and only fragments of the laboratory in which the bipeds had peered at tubes of the deadly red tide. A thin skin of algae and patches of black ooze clung to rocks that once were home only to iguanas.

Occasional terns and boobies still swooped above the waters, and a bevy of penguins dove into the bay at the tribe's approach; although Daniel was again impressed at how well they swam, they looked thin, and Daniel guessed that the fishing was no longer as bountiful as it had been in the past. Even the iguanas seemed in danger of wasting away. No turtles could be seen on the rocky beach; once, it had been full of sand. As the tribe swam the bay, investigating every cranny, a flock of frigates flew from their nesting grounds high on the mountain to hover above the visitors. No one really took notice of the frigates even as they began to dive. It was only when fish mess spattered Daniel that he gazed up to see dozens of red-throats letting go at the tribe with their stinking missiles. Porphyry, as the largest target, took the most direct hits, but fish mess also fouled Percival, Lavender, Nezan, and several others.

"No swim," cawed one of the red-throats. "Get out."

Daniel swiveled his neck to follow that one's flight. "Anna," he called, "doesn't that look like Magellan?"

"I can never tell one of them from another," Anna confessed, "but he is waggling his wings at you."

"No swim! No swim! Get out! Get out!" The frigates continued launching their lunches at the tribe, while their leader screeched his chant. In the bay, the penguins scuttled about, bumping into Daniel's followers as they tried to avoid the pungent projectiles. Lavender and some of the tribe's larger members dove below the surface to wash off the mess, while Goshun and those who were more agile on land washed off and then hauled out of the water onto the lava line. Goshun was annoyed at the birds' antics, and hurled nasty words at them—but Daniel, who had hopped out onto the lava by Goshun's side, watched the sky carefully.

"Get out! Get out! No swim! No swim!" The call echoed again as a second group of frigates wheeled downward and dropped mess not just anywhere, but precisely on those sea mammals who had not yet removed themselves from the waters of the bay. Those on the rocks remained dry.

"Everybody out of the water," Daniel bawled.

"What for?" Goshun barked. "Are you afraid of feathers?"

"Those birds are trying to tell us something," Daniel retorted, his flippers frantically waving at his charges to haul out onto dry land. He slid back in to grab straggling youngsters by the scruff of the neck and shove them onto the lava line. In moments, all who could maneuver on land were out, including Lokat and a few other quite small pups. Porphyry, Lavender, and Percival remained in the water, but, Daniel thought grimly, those flukers could take proper care of themselves.

Having no idea what danger was approaching, Daniel understood that he had been warned out of the water, and thought the warning had come from Magellan—he couldn't be sure at this distance that the lead frigate was Magellan, but he thought it likely. He barked the tribe toward the dense foliage and rocks at the island edge of the lava line, while he clambered onto the highest rock nearby and turned expectantly to view the bay. He didn't have long to wait.

Despite the clarity of the waters, the attackers were nearly invisible as they approached from the surf point. They were under the water and didn't make a sound. Only the frigates had been able to notice them from above. Now, from their slightly elevated position, Daniel and his followers witnessed some lightning-fast kills. A darting penguin was grabbed in midthrust by yawning, gleaming jaws. A sudden boil in the waters threw one of the flightless, black-and-white birds up into the air, and a mottled gray-brown shape leaped out to grasp the penguin on sharklike rows of teeth. All through the bay, a dozen of the beasts snapped and butted and tore their way through a hundred penguins. Very few escaped. The waters swirled with blood and clumps of floating feathers, but still the carnage did not stop.

"Are they snakes?" Anna wondered, drawing back at their ferocity.

"Their heads are snakelike—the jaws that gape so wide, the rows of teeth—but the rest of them looks more like . . ." Daniel trailed off, ashamed of what he wanted to say.

"Like a seal," Agwah finished sadly. "They're more dappled than I am, but otherwise, very much my color and shape."

Daniel shuddered, swallowed, and nodded his head.

"Leopards," said Glex, the red-brown adolescent seal who had spent more time in these southern waters than others in the tribe. "They call 'em leopard seals, with those spots. I never seen one before, but I heard of 'em."

"The lost tribe," Daniel murmured, stunned. He wondered how he'd ever get them to join in his quest. Sitting back on his hind flippers, Daniel watched the leopards leave the bay almost as swiftly and silently as they had entered it, passing Porphyry, Percival, and Lavender on the way out. The fluked members of the tribe were still and silent, pressed against the deep-water end of the lava line. Dismembered carcasses of penguins left behind by the sated leopards littered the surface of the bay. Sharks would have done no more damage to the penguins than these beasts, who were so obviously descended from the Great Beachmaster. Daniel shuddered to think of what would have happened to the tribe's pups if they had been in the bay at the same time as the penguins: They could as easily have died in the snakelike jaws of their "lost" cousins.

In the bay, the remains of the penguins gradually sank bottomward, now food for crabs and fish whose teeth were sharp enough to chip coral. On the rocks at the base of the island, the tribe nuzzled noses with one another, trying to dispel fear. When the attack had been in progress, the frigates had vanished up to their high nesting ground. Daniel considered humping through the jungle to the highlands to talk to Magellan, but decided not to attempt such a difficult journey. If Magellan had anything more to say, he could easily fly down to say it. The frigate bird did not reappear.

Anna, Meeyon, and Marlena chorused their desire to leave the island immediately, afraid for the pups if the leopards should return. Percival and Porphyry expressed no opinion on the matter, and Lavender and Esmeralda were hiding—they, too, ate seals, but only when no fish were to be had, and these southern waters teemed with fish. Daniel refused to panic. "In two nights the moon will be full," he reasoned. "That's when the old turtle should complete her once-each-cycle voyage to the place of her birth. Have we come this close only to turn tail now? We can stick it out for a dozen tides."

~~~~~

Turtle-who-is-a-riddle did not arrive in two days' time, nor in seven. The moon blossomed to full light, slimmed, then became a glimmering shadow. Many seagoing turtles of the correct kind—her offspring, perhaps—returned to pull themselves with flippers onto the barren rocks of the bay and gaze, dull-lidded, this way and that, searching for a beach that no longer existed. But moon's turtle did not come. Daniel spent the days and nights poised at the edge of the lava line, diving in to examine each one's shell as it entered the bay, but did not find what he sought. As each tide lapped on, the tribe grew more restless. Questions surfaced in minds never before troubled by deep thought.

"Why are we here?" Agwah wanted to know. "What good will finding the turtle do?" Wenceslas wondered. "How can a small tribe stop the destruction of the world?" Esther challenged.

The moon was a mere line of curved light and the night was full of thunder and waves of rain when a swift-moving leap tide finally carried into the bay an ancient coldblood of great size. Each limb was as large as one of the seal pups, and her shell could have comfortably held Wenceslas. Daniel slipped into the night waters and swam alongside the turtle toward the shore. There was the grouping, the four representations of the islands! Daniel recognized the pattern and was happy—until he also saw the reason for her delay. Moon's turtle was being choked to death by a ring of clear biped gristle around her neck. She had not so much swum into the bay as been carried in by the currents. Her eyes stared blankly; her flipper movements were torpid. Swiftly Daniel barked instructions, and a half-dozen tribal members entered the waters, some to assist the giant turtle toward the rocky shore, others—Popo with his small head, and Esme with her long teeth—to try to chew the constricting gristle from the turtle's neck in an effort to save her life. Daniel cursed the biped thing. Along their trip to the south, they had passed many bits of the clear stuff that was shaped in rings and floated on the waters. Mothers in the tribe had routinely warned their pups not to play with it. Now it was killing moon's turtle. As she grew—and like all coldbloods she grew constantly, Daniel knew—her neck was choked more and more by the unyielding biped gristle.

Of course, moon's turtle did not understand the intent of her rescuers, or perhaps it was just her will to resist that had kept her alive so long. She fought the helpers with her jaw and powerful flippers. One thrust sent Popo sailing backward and left him unable to breathe for a few moments. Esme grabbed hold of the turtle's shell with her great claws and chewed desperately on the gristle at the back of the turtle's neck as they sank toward the bottom, but to get underneath it for a good grasp of the teeth meant putting pressure on her neck, which would only kill her. The polar bear rolled off.

"Dying anyway," Popo squealed as Goshun and Nezan fastened their teeth onto the turtle's shell and hauled her atop rocks at the base of the bay.

Indeed, the life in the turtle's eyes were fading. Desperately, Daniel searched her grand expanse of shell. The dying Sigmund had spoken of a spot on it that was pulsing red. He found the whorls that were the same as these four islands, and traced with his eyes west, far west, nearly to the shell's edge, until he found a glowing, pulsing red dot. He called Esme and Popo to see—he would have rather had Percy, but there was no time to bring the turtle out into the bay to him.

"Yes, Daniel, I see it," the polar bear cried. The spot seemed to radiate mystery. It had to be Pacifica. But where, precisely, was it located? Why was the moon so slim just when they needed her brightest glow?

A flash of lightning stung the mountaintop like an electric eel's touch—and in its momentary light Daniel saw, around the red spot on the shell, three faint shapes, a group similar to the four in the southern pattern. One was a half-moon, another was a pair of flukes, the third a short flipper bone.

"Did you see those?" Daniel asked Esme and Popo. They nodded solemnly. "Now we have a way to locate Pacifica exactly!"

"Also have trouble," Popo snapped out, turning to look into the bay. Because of their concentration on the turtle—who had now entirely ceased to move—they had not seen what had followed her into the dark, frothing waters. It was the tribe of the leopard seals, and as the last sliver of the moon vanished behind a cloud, reinforcing the darkness of the night, the snakelike cousins churned the waves in angry agitation, as if ready to slice and swallow Daniel and all who swam with him.

Part Two

~~~~~~

PACIFICA FOUND

7

When the Nightblood Blooms

*D*awn was full of splendors, gold and green rays angling skyward before giving way to the molten brilliance of the birthing sun. The beauty of the morning belied the danger facing the tribe. In the bay, a dozen leopard seals swam, silently eyeing the tribal members at the island's base who vied for space with what was left of the penguins and with one very large dead turtle. At the surf point, Porphyry, Percival, and Lavender huddled, near enough to call encouragement to tribal members on the rocks, but unwilling to enter the bay. Daniel imagined a plan in which the shoregoing members would hop along the lava line to where the fluked contingent could form a barrier to protect them from the leopards, but rejected the idea; as the pups traversed the thin line of lava, the leopards might be able to leap up and snatch them from safety. Similar problems made him reject an overland route; once Daniel had taken the tribe up a hill to escape enraged walruses, but there was no hope of climbing the mountain here, nor even of humping along the edge of the island to find a place where the leopards couldn't follow. A dozen more schemes formed and dissolved as Daniel watched the occasional frigate or booby turn high circles above the bay. They did not swoop toward the surface. Smart birds, Daniel thought.

Nezan announced that he, Wenceslas, Goshun, and Glex, four of the largest bulls, were willing to fight the leopards so that the rest of the tribe could escape, even if in fighting they might be killed.

"This wonderful and kind offer demonstrates how very brave each of you is," Daniel told them, "but our main mission is to find Pacifica. To do so, we need the sons of all thirteen lines descended from Saul. If you, Wenceslas, or you, Glex, were to go to sand, we'd be missing a walrus or a red-brown seal, and our mission might not succeed. We can't risk a fight."

"By same reasoning," piped up Popo, "need disgusting leopards, too."

"The lost tribe is found, and must have a place in our band of adventurers," echoed the polar bear.

"I know, I know," sighed the glum Daniel. He limped over to confer with Esme, Popo, and Nezan for some moments, and they listened to the opinions of the three whistlers out by the surf point. All agreed that someone must talk to the loathsome beasts. Daniel had brought the tribe this far, and could not ask anyone else to face the terror. If anything happened to him, the tribe would hop for the lava line and hope for the best. Daniel felt keenly what it meant to have a quest that was more important than his own safety. As he entered the waters, his heart pounded so hard that he was sure the sound must be audible to everyone in the bay.

The leopards slithered near, circled, surrounded him.

Daniel was larger than any single leopard seal bull; the leopards' sinuous strength lay in their numbers. On a shark's first pass, it sniffs to learn the character of the flesh it will sever, but does not attack. That's the time to make your move. One leopard surged within biting distance, and Daniel turned his massive head and crested mane to confront this individual.

"I am Daniel au Fond, sea lion," he began, staring at this first one, and then at others of the cousins. "Son of Tashkent the Terrible, grandson of Whistler Goshun, and great-great-many-times-great-grandson of Beachmaster Saul. I come in peace. My neck is bent to you." Daniel extended his neck in the posture of submission. He had no idea whether the leopards understood what he was saying or the customs of northern pinnipeds, but his neck was not instantly attacked, so he went on.

"I know that you, too, are descendants of the Great Beachmaster, lost to the other races for countless cycles. I bring you greetings from your many cousins. It is easy to see that you are a great race, full of powerful bulls. Perhaps you could destroy me in battle," Daniel admitted. There were hisses from the snakelike leopards at this. "But if you send me to sand," Daniel continued, "there will be sadness upon the waters, and then they will redden with your own blood." The leopards seemed more alert now. Daniel plunged on, hardly stopping for breath. "For I travel in company of other races descended from the Great Beachmaster, and they are more than themselves, too. Beyond each jaw is a hundred others, behind each fin a thousand more. That is because some warriors you see ranged about you on rock and in water are whistlers—whistlers who can call forth the wind to take what happens here to the home coves of many races. Attack me, and you will be hated in the memory of your fellow sea mammals forever!"

When Daniel finished, the silence was broken only by the lapping of waves and the far-off caws of the frigates and booby birds. The leopards flippered quietly just out of biting distance, now and then breaking the surface of the bay with their spotted snouts. Then one swam to face him.

"Sso, ssea lion," the leopard hissed. "Ye ssearch the sseas for sscattered ssons of Ssaul; yet sseeketh ye sserenity, or asssault? Ye inssult our ssovereignty."

"What?"

A gleaming silver dorsal fin surfaced between the leopard seal and the sea lion. "He means you've come proclaiming peace but sounding your challenge to do battle in his territory," Percival translated. "It might be politic to apologize."

"But I offered him my neck."

" 'One must not speak from the mouth and the blowhole at once,' " Percival suggested, quoting an old dolphinic saw.

"I am sincerely sorry," Daniel offered.

"A ssensible ssentiment, sstranger, and ssuitably ssaid."

~~~~~~

Leopards weren't that awful when their jaws were not opened so far that they seemed unhinged, Daniel thought as he, Percival, and the leopard leader trolled the outer reef for a light lunch. Daniel's left foreflipper still bothered him, and he had to swim carefully to avoid bumping into the swiftly turning leopard. The spotted seals not only hissed, they spoke the language in an odd way that Daniel attributed to their having been out of touch with the other races for so many cycles; their speech sounded more like the legend than the way sea mammals now spoke. Even so, Daniel and Percy soon concluded that the leopards had very little understanding of the story of Saul, due, most likely, to their having lost their whistler so long ago that they had no knowledge of true whistlerdom.

"Neither did we sea lions," Daniel admitted. Of even greater interest to Daniel was the name of the leopards' leader: Siwaga. "That's mentioned in the legend!" Daniel said, and addressed him directly. "Members of your tribe must definitely join us in our quest for Pacifica—especially you, Siwaga." He and Percival recited, in chorus, from the verse naming the thirteen sons of Saul:

> *"Siwaga's tears, Porphyry's lament,*
> *Nezan's nose, the eyes of Vaz,*
> *Whatever one wants, the other has."*

" 'Ssiwaga's tearsss?' Ssignify, ssir."

Daniel swallowed. "I thought I'd ask you what it meant." Siwaga was silent, expressionless. "You know—tears? Salty drops that leak out of the eyes when someone cries?"

"Criesss?"

"You know, because of sadness, or hurt, or a loss, or not being understood? Pups do it more, of course, but even adults cry sometimes."

"Sspotted sseals never cry."

"What, never?"

"Abssolutely never."

"Impossible," said Daniel. "Don't you find things sad sometimes?"

Siwaga became angry. "Exisstence iss not ssad, merely harssh," he spat out. "Sspotted livess are nassty and ssevere. Sswim sscores of fathomss in our sskinss before calling uss pariahsss!"

"Swim in your skins? How would we do that?"

Siwaga turned on his hind flippers and started out of the bay.

"The sibilant sachem seems to have something in mind, Daniel," observed Percy. "I think we'd better follow him."

~~~~~

Not everyone in the tribe wanted to do so. Several pinnipeds thought it might be a trap, that Siwaga would lead them to the main group of leopards, who would kill them all. The whistlers, who agreed with Daniel that cajoling the leopards to join the journey to Pacifica was essential, could not entirely lessen the fear of such smaller members as Agwah, Meeyon, and old Esther. But Goshun leaped right into the bay as soon as Daniel barked to the tribe that they were going to follow Siwaga away from Silent Turtle.

"Thanks," Daniel whispered. "I need your support right now, son."

The younger bull grunted. Wenceslas and Glex, who went wherever Goshun did, soon slid into the water, and then the smaller members did, too, following the bulls so they would be protected.

"I smell a test," Nezan intoned as he thrust up near Daniel in the traveling formation. Daniel nodded. Perhaps it would not be as benign as the chase Popo had once led him through the estuarine mud, or the battle with Percival in a kelp bed. All tribes seemed to want to rub a stranger's nose in the muck—or bloody it—before accepting him into their midst.

They were not long away from Silent Turtle when a biped airfloater flew over them, circled, and stayed with the travelers for some time. Daniel looked around, saw the sun glinting off the metal sliver in Palenque's ear, and wondered if it, or perhaps the pouch that still hung from the notch in Lavender's dorsal fin, sent signals to the bipeds so that they could follow his tribe. After a half-tide of open water, the airfloater veered off east toward the unseen continent, and Daniel was relieved. The finned and fluked swimmers coursed south through the day—the first day, Daniel noted, on which they had not passed the drifting, nearly invisible death nets left behind by biped surface floaters. The waters grew cooler. Tonight there would be no moon, and gathering clouds promised severe darkness.

Porphyry and Lavender swam at the rear of the formation, with Nezan and Goshun at the outer points and Wenceslas and Glex just behind Daniel as leader. Thus arrayed, the tribe was a match for any thrust by the leopards, but the spotted ones did not make any move toward an attack in midocean. Percival did a flipper-to-flipper with Siwaga, then came back to report. He seemed happy—but then, his perpetual smile always conveyed that impression.

"We're heading for a dangerous isle where a particular

flower grows, Daniel," Percival said. "Once each cycle, during the thirteen tides when the moon cannot be seen, this flower blooms. It's called the nightblood. Its petals are black, its stem is white, and the fluid in it is black."

"Not my idea of beautiful."

"There's more: The blooms never greet the day, for the nightblood shrivels to ash and dies before true dawn."

"Terrific. They're bringing us all this way to see some silly plant—"

"Don't be rude, Daniel. The spotted seals say that if the nightblood is harvested while it is blooming, the petals are powerful. They can stun any swimmer. But it must be uprooted carefully, or it will kill the harvester."

"What do we need a poison plant for?"

Percival looked at Daniel, shook his head, and then quoted the legend: "*'Death in a flower soon must lie.'*"

Daniel was thunderstruck, and almost stopped swooping his flippers through the water. To make sure, he recited the verse:

> *"Iceberg melt and mountain fly,*
> *Death in a flower soon must lie,*
> *When Pacifica, by evening star,*
> *Greets the wavebender from afar. . . ."*

Plucking a nightblood flower, Percy guessed, had at one time been a test of male maturity for the leopards, and many had died trying to get at it—so many that Siwaga, a sensible swimmer, had all but forbidden the practice. True, the leopards would unquestioningly follow him who could harvest this powerful plant, but Siwaga had issued his challenge to Daniel without knowing the verse of the old legend, though Percival had now sung it for them: Siwaga had simply wanted to frighten Daniel and his tribe into proper respect for the spotted seals' difficult lot in life.

"I respect them already," Daniel groaned. As the traveling formation approached a forbidding isle of uncertain sands and sparse foliage several thousand lengths from the edge of the southern continent, Daniel motioned all the whistlers to him, knowing that surviving this night and harvesting the nightblood was a problem they must solve together.

The tribe beached, the younger animals tumbling to the ground with exhaustion, the mature ones searching out places to rest. In company of Siwaga, Daniel and Esmeralda immediately began to explore. Low and flat, the beach was backed by towering boulders and, off to the side, a plateau on which grew scrawny plants that Daniel did not recognize. The island seemed mostly barren, as if sweet rain seldom settled on its shoulders. Siwaga brought them to the plateau with the scrawny plants. Unlike most plots of land that Daniel had visited, it was bare of brush; on entering it, the leopard dragged his body in a sweep, going around in deliberate circles for a few moments. Generations of spotted leopard seals had done the same, keeping the area clear so that the scrawny plants could bloom into nightbloods.

"But when?" Daniel asked.

"Sslow ssurf," Siwaga answered. Daniel decided that meant long tide, still some time off, and convinced Siwaga to accompany him and Esme to the beach for a ceremony to honor the sun before the important night began.

Dusk flooded the sky quickly, as if the sun were in a hurry to end its daily journey and be eaten by the sea. As it sank into the great ocean and Esme, Daniel, and Siwaga came down from the promontory, all warmth seemed to drain from the remote beach. From an unseen place in the interior of the island, small birdlike animals flew up in a swarm, black against the muted oranges and grays of the evening sky. But they moved in too haphazard a manner to be birds.

"Batss sswoop on ssleeping sseals and ssuck their ssustenance."

"Guess we shouldn't sleep, then," Daniel said nervously, hopping from one foreflipper to the other as they made their way down toward the beach. Siwaga told him more. Bats were known for their soundless approach, for the way they unsheathed their shark-sharp teeth, and for secreting a fluid that allowed them to slice into the skin without awakening the victim and drink blood from noses and other unfurred tissue. Most nights they hunted on the continent, but when leopards were so near, they turned on the seagoers. Several of Siwaga's followers had been sickened and could hardly be woken after being sucked by a bat. That was why, except for the time of the nightblood blooms, leopards avoided this forbidding isle.

On the beach and in the shallows, two tribes gathered. The ceremony was short; Porphyry did not have nearly enough time to sing the complete litany of Saul's praises before the sun had disappeared. Siwaga hurried away toward the plateau. On the beach, Daniel cautioned the bulk of the tribe about sleeping, this night, and then made plans with the whistlers.

By the time Daniel had led Esmeralda, Wenceslas, and Nezan up the twisting path through the brush to the bare, windswept plateau above the beach, night had taken over the sky. There was no moon. Only a few stars could be glimpsed through the cloud cover—one from Saul's fore-flipper, Daniel guessed, though he was not used to the tilt of the Great Beachmaster's outline in the sky this far south and couldn't be certain. The watchers lay on the edges of the clearing, peering at gradations of shadow.

"There," Nezan sniffed, and pointed with his bulbous nose. A half-length in front of them, in the darkness, they saw a scrawny plant that had lost its leaves and now seemed a slender white stalk.

They watched, spellbound, through an entire tide as around the clearing the denuded stalks began to bud. On white, bonelike stems blossomed squid's-ink-black flowers, each with seven delicate petals. Now the plant was beautiful. The sea air was mellow with salt—but the nightblood had no scent. A long-legged crab from the beach reached the plateau and was attracted by the nightblood's bloom; its pincers closed around a pearly stalk, cut it off, and shoved it in its mouth. In a moment, the crab stopped moving, and the bloom sagged over onto it.

Daniel glanced from one to the other of his cohorts and saw fear in each of their eyes. He quietly recited the verse containing the lines about the flower once again, and asked if anyone had any doubt that these were the flowers named in the legend. The massive heads of Wenceslas, Esmeralda, and Nezan shook: no doubt, at all. Even Siwaga concurred.

"Then we've got to get one," Daniel concluded, and set the plan in action. He had dragged a light, workable stick of driftwood to the promontory. With this and Wenceslas's tusks, they sought to dig around a nightblood and remove it from the soil. To prevent the flower from toppling over onto them as they worked, Nezan would interpose his bulk between the walrus and the sea lion and blow at the flower through his nose and cheeks, just hard enough to keep it away from the diggers.

"And I will snatch you back if all else fails," Esme told them. "My claws might be a bit rough on you, but better that than falling into the deadly petals." After they had dug up the plant, Esme, the only creature among them who could move solely on her hind legs, would carry it down to the beach, where it would be put into the pouch that Lavender still carried.

The digging was difficult, and took much longer than Daniel had imagined possible. He and Wenceslas had to time their thrusts to the breaths of Nezan, and of course the walrus had to restrain his own natural enthusiasm so as not to let his skin touch the plant, to use only his solid tusks. His group must have made quite a sight to a bat, Daniel thought—the bulky walrus, sea-lion bull, and elephant seal hugging the earth, working with tusk and stick at a black-petaled bloom, watched over by the towering white polar bear and the slithering leopard seal.

Just before dawn, the task was done. The last of the roots came away from the earth and the nightblood toppled slowly over on its side, free. Daniel and Wenceslas hurriedly backed away, and Nezan remained in position.

"Good job, everyone. Time to go," Daniel said. But Nezan didn't move. Daniel hurried to look at him. His eyes still showed some life, but his huge head with its bulbous nose seemed frozen in place.

"Ssniffed in ssome petal-dusst. Unlesss he spews it, he'll perissh!"

Esmeralda was about to use sticks and brush to pick up the plant and its trailing roots, but stopped. She bent down and pulled up a particularly fragrant clump of brush, then delicately inserted it into the space between the fallen nightblood and Nezan's nose. In a moment, Esme was rewarded with a slight twitch of the bulbous appendage. Nezan was alive!

Daniel was all set to let out a victory whoop when the elephant seal reared back his head and was rocked by an explosive sneeze. After it, he slowly rose up on his flippers and shook the cobwebs from his brain. But Daniel looked around and saw that the precious nightblood was gone. He almost panicked, but a chorus of surprised barks from below alerted him to what had happened: The power of Nezan's nose's exhalation had blown the frail bloom over the edge of the promontory, whence it had wafted down and landed on the beach, in sight of the rest of the tribe, but without hitting any of the members. That was fortunate, because though its power diminished when it was out of the earth, it could have killed one of the smaller pups.

"Huh," Esme said. "Saved me the trouble of carrying it down." They had a good laugh over that.

Scampering to the beach, they found an elated tribe. The excitement had scared away the bloodsucking bats. One by one the leopard seals, including Siwaga, came over to Daniel, bent their necks, and pledged to swim with him to the end of the oceans.

"That's where we're planning to go," he told them.

Working to beat the approach of dawn, Esme and Daniel maneuvered the poisonous plant, roots, clinging earth, and all to the pouch that Lavender carried. The biped thing dangled from her left fluke, and Esme's teeth and claws fastened it tight.

"Nothing else made by a biped ever did us any good," Goshun said.

"You're right, son, but remember that the legend holds that Pacifica cannot be fathomed *'until Kanonah's pups do sea lions tell.'* That means the bipeds have to communicate with us."

"Hmph."

The beachmaster loped into the waters. "To Pacifica," he sang. "We know where to go, we are eleven of the thirteen lines descended from Great Saul, and we're in shape to travel fast."

8

At the Lip

They coursed west, due west, the forbidden direction, toward the end of the waters, the place where every evening the sun was eaten by the sea. On the journey, all was stripped away from Daniel, even the pretense of command: In an ocean this vast and devoid of land there seemed no need for leadership. The tribe swam, ate, slept, and progressed toward an uncertain goal, flesh in motion, with few thoughts troubling the mind. Conversations started and then slacked off into silence and rhythmic flipper or fin strokes, while the tribe stared at clouds or searched the waters below for some sight to relieve the monotony.

When the smaller animals were weary, Porphyry or Lavender simply carried them for a while. It was a treat to see an exhausted sea-lion pup clutching the killer whale's dorsal fin as she sped along, carefully swimming so that her fin stuck out of the water, which allowed the little one curled to it to sleep more comfortably.

Daniel worried that they had not yet become thirteen. Where was Cendrillon the manatee? Or a narwhal to take the place of Diarmuid, long ago torn apart by jealous walruses? Nothing in the legend spoke of requiring thirteen tribes; nonetheless, he felt it as a pressing need. And yet the tribe could not have waited near Cracked Egg for Cendrillon to arrive. The turtle's death made it clear there was not much time in which to rediscover Pacifica. The world was in dusk. How much longer before it would submerge in full night?

The boredom of the days was broken only by hunting. The leopards and such sizable animals as Lavender required a lot of food, and in these vast open seas there was little to be found; Daniel feared that in their hungry frenzies the big eaters might by mistake attack a smaller member of the tribe. That didn't happen in a quarter-moon of traveling, but when the tribe located a school of a thousand orange-skinned scalers of about half-flipper size, Lavender, Siwaga, and experienced animals such as Esmeralda and Wenceslas gorged themselves. No one had ever seen these before, but they tasted crisp and sweet, and caused no discomfort after eating. The tribe chased and bit and gulped and chewed with complete abandon. Shortly afterward, the sated swimmers floated in the half-daze that often came in the wake of a too-full meal. Not a single fish of the school was left alive. Daniel, too, had eaten a large share, but viewing the waters he shuddered: It was sea-lion custom always to graze cautiously on a fat school, regardless of the strength of the growls in one's stomach, to leave enough fish alive so that the school could replenish itself in time for a tribe's next transit of the same waters. But these were unusual waters and unusual times. If a day became too hot or a night too long and a battle seemed to loom, say, between Siwaga's leopards and the northern dappled seals, the whistlers would call for a six-tide fast, or challenge pairs of potentially opposing warriors to match strokes and imagine life as the other swam it. Such stratagems invariably altered the moods of would-be combatants and kept the tribe of one mind as they aimed west.

Daniel's mood was altered by bottom-scouting excursions with the elephant seal Nezan, who was now kin. No animal could dive as deep as the big-nosed bull, and he sometimes took Daniel with him on these jaunts. As they entered the darkest depths, Daniel felt an urge to close his eyes, for they could no longer see anything anyway. Nezan told him that was exactly what was to be done, to shut down the parts of the body that were useless at such depths, and to rely on the others. Daniel swam deep and closed his eyes. He felt a great sense of going forward, of swimming effortlessly without willing it, of aligning himself with rather than against such forces as the north wind and the swirling bottom sands. When he told Nezan of this feeling, the big nose bobbed up and down in agreement.

"And it's hopeless to try to explain it to the others," Nezan growled. "They'd only laugh."

"And you don't like laughter," Daniel teased.

"Life is a joke only to those who fight it," Nezan observed.

"Ride the wave, don't go through it?"

"Yes."

Once in a while, during the tides of the sun, the noise of a biped airfloater would be heard coming from the east, and then the giant metallic bird itself would appear over-head, glinting with the sun's reflection. It would circle the tribe a half-dozen times, then fly off again whence it had come, staying in view a long time before vanishing. Daniel wondered if the bipeds were following the tribe because of the metal thing in Palenque's ear, or because Lavender might well be carrying some unknown device on her body or in the sack the bipeds had fastened to her during captivity. The presence of bipeds trailing the tribe was un-settling, but at least it was evidence that the tribe had a common enemy.

"Such a conclusion is an occlusion," Percival counseled him.

"What are you spouting, dolphin?" Daniel responded. Percy never used a small word when he could find a big one.

"Pacifica was home cove to bipeds as well as sea mammals."

"Well, you're right about that," Daniel allowed. "To think of the two-leggeds as enemies may close a passage that must be opened."

Percival trilled and clicked with pleasure, and did a quick roll.

"Nonsense," Goshun grumbled. "It's fine to say bipeds are needed, but I've never known one that really helped us."

"Fred," Daniel said quickly. "My trainer."

"Aw, Dad—he kept you in captivity for many moons," Goshun protested, slapping a wave in anger.

"Later he came to regret that, I believe."

"You don't really know that he didn't want to hurt you.

You're just guessing—projecting real emotion on bipeds when you don't even know definitely that they *have* feelings," Goshun spat out.

<center>~~~~~</center>

The moon in the daytime sky grew her full coat and then shed it steadily until it was only a sliver of light difficult to see. Just when it seemed as if the featureless sea would never end, an airfloater appeared at the horizon and approached the tribe—from the west. In the manner of the others, it circled and then flew back in the direction from which it had come.

"Pacifica is near," Daniel exclaimed, and told the tribe why: Such airfloaters had homes only on land, so there must be land not far away. They swam with renewed energy. Two days later land birds flew overhead, and after one day more, faint brown smudges appeared on the western horizon. Daniel's heart was in his mouth as he directed the tribe slowly to swim the perimeter of what seemed to be three islands set in a semicircle that faced south. One had the shape of a moon ripped in half, the second was fluked, and the third resembled a short flipper bone such as could sometimes be found whitening on the sea floor. This pattern of three matched that on the turtle's back, and the tribe realized they had entered the turquoise waters of Pacifica and cried with joy.

But the journey was not complete. Because the turtle had been small in relation to the vastness of the ocean, the pattern on its shell told only that the ancient home cove was in the vicinity of these three islands. They looked so ordinary. Lush and green, the half-moon was full of vegetation and had a small colony of bipeds on one beach. The flukes seemed entirely barren; no life was visible, though coral grew rampant near shore. Mountains could be seen atop the flipper bone, an island overrun with bipeds whose dwellings Daniel spied everywhere in the vegetation. He wondered if the high point on Short Flipper Bone was where Saul had deposited Kanonah when the rains ceased and the waters began to recede.

"Wow! Greatest surf ever!" exclaimed little Lokat, eyes gleaming. He and the other youngsters were excited because Short Flipper Bone did indeed have long, high, curling waves of cresting power that careened a full hundred lengths before collapsing off the glistening white beach. Daniel's attention was caught more by a different sight: another of those offshore shelves that the bipeds seemed to be implanting all over the earth to take things from the sea. Didn't they have enough territory of their own? This shelf was somewhat different in appearance. It swarmed with the two-leggeds and was surrounded by floaters.

"Where do you think the entrance of Pacifica is?" Nezan inquired.

"I feel it strong and close," Esmeralda muttered. "But the presence of the bipeds confuses the senses."

"I don't think the bipeds know about Pacifica," Daniel said.

"Then what are they doing here?" Goshun wondered.

To find out, they headed under the surface of the waters.

A few moments of swimming at two dozen lengths down revealed the true features of the land and seascape. The biped shelf was rooted by its metal legs on the top of an undersea mountain, at a depth at which light from the sun was already faint. Undersea valleys spread from this mountain in several directions, their true bottoms hidden in darkness. It dawned on Daniel that the islands were the tips of neighboring sea mounts, and that all of them were connected underneath by the valleys. Many bipeds and their machines were in the water. You seldom found a biped without a machine near, Daniel mused. Bipeds in sea-lion coverings rode undersea carriers that looked like upended turtle shells toward a central device twined about the legs of the shelf. There, the bipeds transferred the contents of the turtle shells—jagged pieces of the sea floor—onto a machine that, starfishlike, fed its food up toward the belly of the shelf. This was not a machine for taking the ooze out of the bottom of the sea, but a machine for taking chunks of the bottom and doing something with them.

Percival was most fascinated by the firelights that the biped swimmers bore with them, for they seemed to burn and pierce the darkness like tiny suns. "How can there be fire under water?" he wondered to Daniel as they tried to stay hidden behind a boulder.

Daniel had no answer. They swam down, in the direction from which the turtle shells were approaching the machine. A hundred lengths distant, they saw bipeds working intently on the dark sea floor, but did not get close enough to them to figure out what they were doing. As a turtle shell passed, a medium-sized chunk of what the bipeds had harvested fell off, knocked against a boulder, and broke apart. Daniel investigated. Something inside the rock glinted with light reflected from the fire-bearing sticks: something the color of the sun.

"Gold," Percival whispered.

Daniel had seen that color inside rocks before, but never so much of it in one rock. He directed the tribe to stay down near the bottom, and out of the bipeds' sight—not an easy task for Porphyry the baleen, because of his great bulk, and impossible for Esmeralda, Popo, and Palenque, who were unable to remain underwater for a long time without breathing. Daniel soon sent the polar bear and otters back up, accompanied by the smallest pups, whose undersea capacity had not yet become well developed. Flippering closer to where the bipeds were working, Daniel saw that all of the bipeds were suddenly moving away from a place on the floor where a large hole had recently been dug. Moments later, there was a puff of flame and shocks of sound blasted Daniel's ears and sensitive whiskers, temporarily stunning him. The sea lion whirled and searched the depths for Porphyry, knowing from past experience that the larger the body in the way of an explosion, the greater the consequences. The great baleen swayed in the currents and seemed lost, but indicated to Daniel that he was intact. Daniel did not want to lose such a large warrior at a time like this, but Porphyry insisted on staying. The baleen was more of a hindrance than a help just then, but Daniel understood that he wanted to be present at this important moment. Porphyry's time would come, Daniel thought. The pain in Daniel's flipper reminded him to keep to his goal no matter what the consequences.

After the dust and rocks settled back to the sea floor,

the bipeds went back to the spot where they had made the explosion. Daniel could see that large boulders had been split into chunks of a size that could now be loaded onto the turtle shells, and that a deep gouge had been cut into the bottom. Investigating, Daniel was drawn beyond the site of the biped activity, further into the depths of the undersea valley, where the explosion had produced great upheaval in the sea floor. The tribe followed. As they coursed downward, the sea warmed.

He seemed lured by something in the far depths, faintly glimmering in the darkness. He flippered onward, even though the water was becoming uncomfortably warm, and there it was: a boulder more perfect than any of the others, narrow and upright, illumined at a dozen points all over its body by light reflected from the now distant fire-bearing sticks. Fortunately, the bipeds had not yet happened upon it. Going closer, he realized that the object was newly released from the sea floor, for no coral grew on it, nor were its contours unduly rounded as they would have been from long exposure to the currents. It was almost straight. Then he saw something even more astounding on the boulder: concentrations of gold that seemed denser than the natural seams they saw in other pieces of the sea floor, along with traces of indentations in the rock. "*Gold of understanding*," he thought. Could it really be that?

"Glex," he called to the red-brown seal, whose whiskers were much longer than anyone else's, "can you brush the sand off that boulder without upsetting it?" Glex brushed carefully for a few moments, and then Daniel took another look. His heart jumped. Now the concentrated gold and accompanying cracks in the boulder formed the outlines of a sea mammal and a biped. They were blurred, but nonetheless distinct.

Pacifica was real, and after thousands of cycles had been found again by the descendants of Great Saul.

At his moment of triumph, his heart thundering, Daniel flippered aside to allow the members of the tribe to file past and view the boulder with their own eyes. As the tribal members gazed at the boulder, Daniel spotted what seemed to be a pair of shining lights approaching through the dark seas toward the gold-encrusted rock. The shape moved closer. It was as large as Porphyry, shaped much the same, but with a skin of metal. It moved through the dark waters by means of a whirler at its tail. As it neared, Daniel could see that in addition to the two lights, there were eyeholes and two gigantic claws at the head or front. A biped object, a metal baleen. This was a place of wonders. Could the metal baleen be connected with the gold-harvesting operation?

"Disregard the biped thing. We must pursue Pacifica," Percival reminded Daniel even as they both warily eyed the intruder.

"But in which direction?" Daniel asked.

"Follow the heat," Percival advised.

Daniel acknowledged the logic of that guess and ordered the tribe into battle lines, Siwaga and his leopard seals arranged as scouts forward of the teardrop formation. They proceeded further into the depths of the valley. The heat grew in intensity, causing discomfort. Some swimmers were cough-choking with the strange smells in the water.

It was of some comfort that the biped metal baleen was no longer in sight.

They swam along a ridge toward a crevice that seemed to lead into the heart of the earth. Seething clouds bubbled from it, clouds that contained bits of rock. Here was the source of the heat, Daniel felt, and of the rock clusters on the sea floor that contained gold. Geysers spewed out the rocks from deep within the earth. There were beautiful red terraces and shimmering water. Colonies of giant white tube worms topped with blood-red plumes waved in the undersea breeze, amid cones of rock of the sort seen in caves, cones that gave off bubbles when a swimmer knocked against one. A fish swam by, as long as a flipper but with a huge mouth, sharp fangs, blue eyes, and front legs.

"Ugliest fish I ever saw," Goshun allowed. Then he saw another one with a tail like a manta ray, and a clam with blue muscles.

Geysers rose up from the ocean floor, spewing thick water full of metal and minerals. The crevice was so hot that Daniel shrank from it. Even if this was the entrance to Pacifica, how could the tribe ever go deeper? If they went any farther, they would be burned alive.

No sooner had he come to that conclusion than the crevice disgorged monsters.

Scaly, squidlike, and deathly white, with stalked eyes like those of crabs, they loomed up from the depths by the dozens, each the size of a leopard seal. Daniel knew they weren't monsters, but creatures from the depths who never saw the light of day. They were terrifying, so transparent that you could see their organs through their skins; they even carried their own light with them—knobs on their arms that seemed to shine in the dark waters. In a flash, Daniel also understood the old legend's tale of Kratua, guardian of Pacifica, whose breath turned the ocean to flame: These creatures didn't breathe fire, but came from the depths where fire was. And there were many of them—like a monster with many heads. Before Daniel could get out a warning not to provoke the Kratuans, a leopard seal lunged to attack with his jaw unhinged and his rows of teeth exposed. The waters roiled as several creatures swarmed on the leopard and he disappeared under their onslaught. It was all over in a moment. Each pale attacker carried a piece of the victim—his blood indistinguishable from the black waters—down into the crevice, and others swam to take their places. Enraged, Siwaga sought revenge and was joined in battle by Lavender, her white underside flashing in the darkness. Between them, they managed to kill a transparent creature, but of course they wouldn't eat such a strange thing. However, the other beasts grabbed and ate the dead one, their stalked eyes quivering with each snap of their jaws.

At least that proved the creatures were mortal, Daniel thought. But an immediate all-out attack would surely result in the destruction of the tribe, which he could not allow.

"Swim up and away," he shouted.

Siwaga hissed that they could counter the attack, but Lavender understood and shouldered past the leopard, aiming for the surface. Most of the tribe followed her gladly, and Daniel urged on the stragglers. As they streaked up and away, they passed the metal baleen, still in the vicinity of the upright boulder encrusted with gold.

The Kratuans broke off their pursuit of the tribe, and turned to attack the metal baleen.

"Don't stop to look!" Daniel shouted, and urged his followers upward until light from the sun could be felt and seen. The Kratuans were still in the depths, and there was no sign of the metal baleen. Daniel was thankful for the tribe's escape, but in agony. At the very lip of Pacifica, they were unable to get in.

9

Until Kanonah's Pups Do Sea Lions Tell

The tribe sprawled on a white-sand beach and in the shallows of the crescent-shaped island, Riven Moon. Behind them lay dense vegetation, palm and coconut fronds waving in gentle breezes above spiky underbrush. Offshore, majestic white-crested seas marched toward their break point, where they cried aloud and bowed their necks to the land before giving up their power. The moon had vanished, and no longer competed with the sun for space amidst the clouds.

Daniel had brought the tribe here after their encounters in the depths. Now he must figure a way past the transparent guardians and the intense heat to enter Pacifica. It was difficult for him to think about formidable tasks, though, when the surroundings were so beautiful, the sun was relaxing his muscles, and the wind was lightly ruffling his fur.

Not far away on the beach was a colony of bipeds. The greater concentration of that race was on Short Flipper Bone, but a small group had spread their machines and playthings along a rock outcropping. They pointed metal and glass tubes upward, looking at the sun. Daniel wondered why, since the sun was easily seen with one's eyes. At least these descendants of Kanonah seemed content to ignore his tribe, who lay exposed and exhausted.

While their tubes were focused on the sky, the bipeds were distracted by the arrival of another group, who came by floater. Towed behind the big floater was the metal baleen. Now Daniel could see definitely that it was a biped carrier, for at a spot where the dorsal fin should have been, part of the cover rose up and two bipeds emerged from inside.

The bipeds transferred the metal baleen to a wooden enclosure at the edge of the water, and soon after began to use spark-throwing sticks on the metal skin of the baleen, which had dents and scars in it. Although Daniel wondered what the two-leggeds were doing, he had to return his mind to the main task. He splashed into the waters to confer with the whistlers about Pacifica.

The boulder had definitely been a signal for an entryway, they all agreed. But how could that be, when Pacifica was supposed to have been at the junction of land and water? Daniel thought that the spot had once been above water and was now below it.

Nezan chimed in to suggest that the upheavals were still going on. "Kratuans resemble bottom dwellers who never rise to sunlit levels," he stated, and since he had the most experience in going to the greatest depths, the others accepted that reasoning.

"So they don't like sunlight, is that it?" Daniel asked.

"Yes."

"But we've still got to get through their territory."

Lavender, lolling in the surf and almost beached, suggested using the nightblood flowers in her sack to stun or kill the squidlike guardians.

"Might not work on strange beasts," Popo said, shaking his body. He had a hard time staying in one place because of the undertow.

"Might kill us, too," Esmeralda said as she kept her fur wet to protect it from the balmy air of this area of the ocean. Nonetheless, they decided to loose the nightbloods on the Kratuans, but only if there were no other way to deter the beasts.

"And what of Kratua's breath that turns the sea to fire?" Percival asked. They knew, now, that this description from the legend was not strictly true, but only figuratively so; yet the problem remained. How could they withstand the great heat coming from the chasm of the apparent entrance to Pacifica? No one had an answer for Percy's query. They had no way to get past the heat of the crevice, and decided not to make another attempt to enter Pacifica until they had a way to counter the heat.

Next day, from the direction of Short Flipper Bone, an airfloater appeared in the sky. It seemed similar to the one that had been following them at intervals during their journey toward Pacifica, and it soon glided downward and alit on the surface of the waters near where the tribe was perched. Using its whirler, it drew alongside the wooden nesting place of the metallic baleen, the undersea floater. Several bipeds climbed out of the airfloater onto a landing place, and one walked across the sands in the direction of the tribe; two more followed cautiously.

Daniel thought he recognized the one in the lead as his old trainer Fred, but couldn't be sure. Others in the tribe watched the slow and deliberate approach of the humans. The leader wore glass over his eyes and his beard had tinges of gray. He came within five lengths of Daniel. Any closer and the entire tribe will flee toward the water, Daniel thought—but the biped seemed to know that, too. He stopped at the correct distance and made the hand signal for "Hello."

Now there could be no doubt: This biped was Fred. Daniel had been taught the greeting signal and many others, moons ago when a captive in the biped laboratory. Daniel didn't immediately respond to Fred, but barked to the tribe, "I know this biped. Do not be alarmed."

Assured by their leader, the tribe relaxed a bit. Popocatepetl guessed that one of the other visitors looked like a biped who had lived in the shelf above his tribe in the estuary. And Lavender thought she recognized the third biped as one who had fed her extra fish in the cove where she had been confined. Neither Popo nor Lavender could be certain of the identifications because, as Popo put it, "All bipeds look alike."

Since all three bipeds had stepped out of the same airfloater, Daniel countered by saying that they were not all alike. "Each of these three, for whatever reasons, has been following us for some time," he pointed out. "They're certainly being respectful. Maybe they've even realized that sea mammals don't *like* bipeds."

"That would be a first," Goshun grumbled. "They usually think all animals are interested in them, and try to make us do what they do—shake flippers, or balance their toys on our noses. Their pride puffs up bigger than Nezan's nose sack, and it never comes down to normal size."

"Watch those jokes, Junior," Nezan smiled.

"Bipeds don't care that *we* have to live in the seas," Goshun went on. "They think it's only their territory." Strong murmurs of assent rose from the rest of the tribe, including Nezan. To Daniel, Goshun's anger, the aura of ice-blue around him, grew brighter as he spoke of the bipeds in terms Daniel remembered using when younger. Goshun cited as evidence of biped pride the slaughters of the pups in the far north, the terrible assaults on the whales in the southern archipelago, the drift-net fishing that caught up all sea creatures in its path, the many kinds of waste and ooze that the tribe had passed in nearly every cove and even on the wide oceans.

As Goshun continued on in this vein and moved away from the three bipeds, the tribe edged in his direction. At the same time, Fred and his companions responded to calls from their kind who were near the metallic baleen, and went over to that. Leaving the tribe, Daniel loped cautiously over the sands toward the big metallic thing to get a better look. There was a bit of a stir from the bipeds as he approached, but Fred said something to them and the two-leggeds moved out of his way.

Impaled on a claw of the metal baleen was the limp body of a Kratuan squid. The dents in the head part probably had been made by Kratuans attacking the vehicle. Fred moved his hand to touch the monster, and Daniel instinctively barked a warning and made a flipper signal for "Danger."

Fred stepped back from the Kratuan, and smiled.

They had a reunion then, a respectful one that was also a bit frustrating for Daniel. They could communicate only by the limited language of flipper signals—a fact that brought to mind the last time he and Fred had seen one another. That was when Sigmund the orangutan lay dying on Silent Turtle Island, smashed in the great wave. Sigmund had been their link, able to talk to Daniel in the language of animals and, by means of his supple hands, to convey more to and from the bipeds than flipper signals could. At Sigmund's death, brought together by the loss of a common friend, Fred and Daniel had cried and touched.

Fred had originally been Daniel's captor in the laboratory where Daniel and other pinnipeds—and Sigmund—had been challenged with puzzles. When Daniel had demonstrated that his brain was as supple as his neck, which could swivel his head in all directions, Fred had almost ceased to be a captor and had taught Daniel many useful things. After Daniel had escaped and returned to the open sea, Fred had shown up in Daniel's life at odd times. For instance, several cycles ago, Fred had thrown exploding firesticks at pursuing bipeds to enable Daniel to lead Tashkent and some others out of the old home cove. Last cycle, in the southern archipelago, Fred had aided Zelda and little Blossom when they were near death from the ravages of the red tide. Daniel thought that Fred had become almost a pinniped, or, more precisely, had matured to the point of acting less like a biped and more like a mammal who had proper respect for other beings.

Daniel was trying to find a way to communicate to Fred an idea he had, when there was a great commotion further down the beach. Fred scurried to take part in it. The bipeds were pointing their long tubes at the sun and exhibiting great excitement. For a moment Daniel did not know why, but then the impossible happened.

The sun started to disappear from the sky.

The moon—completely absent from the lofty regions only moments before—was biting the sun, taking a chunk from the side of the fiery circle. Daniel hurried to his tribe, gazing upward as he loped along the sands. At each gallop, the sky seemed to darken more and more. How could the moon appear in full coat, when just a night or two earlier she had completely shed her bright coat? Overnight the moon had grown to the size of the sun! Was the sun dying? Nezan, Popo, and the other whistlers on the beach trembled and began murmuring and chanting, half-closing their eyes against the terrible sight. Off to the east of the moon, darkness was following on its trail as a black cloud follows the octopus that spews it. With incredible swiftness, night was filling the sky. Stars began twinkling, even the eye-star of the Great Beachmaster.

"Save us from the end of the world, O Great Saul," Percival sang plaintively from the shallows, his cry echoed by Lavender and Porphyry, who thrashed about in the surf. Daniel had never seen them so frightened.

Porphyry groaned and shuddered.

"What's the matter, great one?"

"The sun and the moon are mating/and the earth below is shaking," the big baleen moaned. Even as he had lain in the shallows, his sensitive ears had picked up some vibrations from under the sea. Daniel didn't know what they might be, nor if they were connected to the event in the sky. The agony of the whistlers increased as the moon took more and more of the sun, and darkness flowed over the sea and the island.

"Why are the whistlers so scared, Daniel?" Anna asked him, shouldering near. "The legend says Pacifica cannot be found '*until the sun in darkness dwell*,' and it is certainly going into darkness now."

"That's it!" Daniel nuzzled her gratefully. It was the fulfillment of another condition of the "until" verse of the legend. They watched the darkening sun together. In a few moments, the moon would almost completely cover her male companion in the sky. But Daniel felt no ill effects, only a slight cool breeze in the air. His heart beat. His limbs moved when he willed them to. None of the animals in his tribe seemed in danger of dying. Little Lokat was even sleeping through all the commotion.

The middle part of the sun was entirely dark, though occasional bright bursts of fire flared at its edges. Daniel stared at the sun and moon, and so did all the other beings on the beach, sea mammal and biped. The clash in the sky drew the eyes of all. Here was such power and majesty that a wavebender must savor it, even though in the beauty of this sky-bursting embrace most sensed the sharp taste of danger.

As he watched the sun living in darkness, Daniel suddenly knew what to do about the last unfulfilled condition of the "until" verse, "*Until Kanonah's pups do sea lions tell.*"

He, the descendant of Beachmaster Saul most imbued with the great forefather's spirit, would have to communicate with Fred, a many-times-great-grandson of the biped chieftain Kanonah. Though for countless generations sea lions had thought of bipeds as the enemy, Daniel would have to share his quest with Fred, somehow enlist Fred's aid in entering the long-drowned home cove. The metallic baleen, not being flesh, could withstand the intense heat coming from the crevice and carry Daniel and Fred into Pacifica. Yes! It made sense: In Pacifica, once, bipeds and sea lions had lived in harmony; now the two races must together enter the ultimate secret place.

The moon tired of her position atop the sun and began to move aside. Flashes of brilliance peeped out from behind her, their dazzling rays occasioning shouts of relief from the beach. In another few moments the sun's intensity overwhelmed the frail moon and thrust her toward oblivion. She began to vanish. Daniel fervently hoped that when night came again the moon would reappear in her more usual haunts.

When she was entirely gone, it was as if she had never been in the daytime sky. In fewer moments than it took to swim from one beach to another, it seemed as if an entire night had gone by. It was as if time itself had been sped up—a sensation that reminded Daniel forcefully of what happened to time during his battle with the sand- and wind-monsters throughout his training sessions on Bird's Neck, and while on his deep dives with Nezan.

Perhaps that explained why, when the other animals recovered quickly from watching the odd sky event, the whistlers did not do so as easily; Popo, Percy, Porphyry, Nezan, and the usually unflappable Esmeralda cowered on the beach and in the shallows. They were, after all, the most sensitive animals, and perhaps Daniel should have expected their incapacity. Suddenly he felt exposed, his protectors taken from him by an unforeseen happening. He wanted to consult with them about his plan, but they were in no mood to hear him. Yet he had to act quickly. It was impossible to tell how long the sandbar of opportunity would remain above water.

He loped quickly to Fred and tried to make him understand that he wanted to go in the metallic baleen to the bottom of the sea and enter the chasm that led to Pacifica. It was immensely difficult to convey this by means of hand signals. He had to use the signs for such expressions as "Come," "Open," "Go fetch," and "Good job," and it took a long time, but Fred proved supple enough to acknowledge that Daniel wanted to get into the vehicle—now. "Yes," Fred signed. Whether Fred understood more than that, Daniel couldn't be certain. To tell Fred what Pacifica was, and what it meant to the sea mammals, seemed completely beyond hand and flipper signals.

Fred turned to talk to some of the other bipeds, who seemed skeptical. Daniel decided he couldn't help Fred with the task of convincing the biped tribe, and went back to his own. The whistlers were recovering—the smaller ones more quickly than Porphyry or Lavender—and Daniel told them he was going to go in the metal baleen, which he hoped could withstand the heat, and somehow open the entrance of Pacifica. The others could slipstream behind the vehicle and perhaps in that way be protected from the heat.

"And from the Kratuans?" Goshun wondered.

"We'll use the nightbloods on them," Daniel responded.

Goshun let out a loud bark of disdain.

"Of course it's a risk," Daniel insisted. "But there's no other way. Sometimes you have to take risks or you'll never really accomplish the goal."

"I go with you," Popocatepetl piped up.

Daniel thought about this offer. He would have preferred Percival as a helper, because Percy had the best mind of all of them, but Percy couldn't function well out of the water, and there would be no water inside the metal baleen. "Not take up much room," Popo said.

"Okay, okay."

Daniel glanced at Anna. There were no questions in her eyes. She knew this was the right thing to do, and nodded so. Reassured, Daniel loped toward the bipeds, followed by the little otter.

———

The vehicle was so cramped that Daniel and Popo had to lie almost flat, near Fred and the second biped who was making it go. Once under the surface, they kept their eyes focused through the glass in front on the depths beyond. Daniel wondered if this was what it felt like to be Porphyry, or a turtle inside his own shell. Had Kanonah felt this way when he was in Saul's belly for a cycle? The second biped in the metallic baleen kept turning around to stare at Daniel and Popo, as if he couldn't believe they were inside with him, and steadily emitted a scent of fear.

Fred and his companion inside the vehicle wore sea-lion coverings. The shells dangled from the sides of their faces. The baleen passed places on the sloping sea floor where other bipeds in such coverings were making small explosions in the sea bottom. These, Daniel saw, detached some of the gold-bearing rocks from the floor so that the bipeds could load them onto the tentacles of the big machine that fed up into the shelf. The impact of the blasts jolted the vehicle as it moved beyond the workers and toward the site of the upright boulder and the crevice.

By soft barks and nudges to Fred, Daniel urged the vehicle in the direction of the boulder. In the distance it gleamed, reflecting the light-throwers on the front of the carrier. The darkness became more intense as they sank lower and lower. Behind them, Daniel could sense rather than see, the tribe was following. He barked to Fred to veer about so he could see the tribe. They seemed to be encountering less difficulty than on the previous dive. Maybe the heat coming from the crevice was less than it had been; that could mean that the earth was still moving. Daniel hoped the tribe would be able to stay down in the depths. No Kratuans had yet appeared, and he was thankful for that.

They neared the boulder with the markings on it. Daniel indicated that this was the spot. Examining the boulder by means of the light-throwers, Fred became excited. He seemed to want to maneuver the metal baleen into position to grasp at the boulder with its claws. Daniel tried to tell Fred this must not be done, but Fred just grinned and made the hand signal for "Good job."

This was all wrong! Daniel barked loudly, the sound

hurting even his own ears in this tightly confined space.

"Should I bite him?" Popo asked.

There wasn't time to answer. As the carrier's claws reached the marked boulder, the creatures from the depths appeared and began to attack, slamming their bodies against the metallic sides. Inside, sea mammals and bipeds alike were jostled and tossed together. Even worse, the force with which the Kratuans rammed the vehicle made the claws fastened around the boulder push it from its already precarious position. It started to topple, and that caused great spouts of sand and debris to erupt from the sea floor.

Chaos. Through the eye-places of the metal baleen, Daniel caught glimpses of the bulls and the Kratuans in combat.

"The nightbloods! Release the nightbloods!" he shouted, but his words did not carry beyond the confines of the metal shell.

"Aaagh," Popo cried, as he saw Palenque in the grasp of a transparent squid. She bit off one of its eyes and wriggled away, but she was hurt. Popo clawed at the glass to get to her, but could not.

Crack! The sound exploded through the vehicle and water started to gush in through the glass of the front. Daniel looked up and saw that the boulder had fallen on the metal baleen.

Fred and the other biped screamed and grabbed head-coverings and face-shells as the vehicle filled with water that rushed in so quickly it split the baleen's sides. Daniel and Popo were flung out, Daniel's flipper pierced by jagged metal. He ignored the hurt. Screaming to Goshun to release the nightbloods from the sack at Lavender's back, he rushed to ram one of the transparent squids that was nearing Fred. Deflecting the attack, Daniel gave Fred time to place his shell properly over his nose and mouth. The monster turned toward Daniel, and he flippered backward. Percival appeared and ripped it through with his long, smiling jaw. Daniel could see Esme's claws undoing the sack at Lavender's dorsal fin.

Nightblood petals floated like shining black eyes in the whirling sands near the fallen boulder. A Kratuan snapped one up and went into immediate spasms. Others among the monsters aimed for the floating petals, lured by their intense blackness. The Kratuans seemed incapable of not snapping at anything in their path, friend or foe.

Turning to search for Fred, Daniel caught only a glimpse of the biped flippering up and away. He hoped Fred would be safe, but could pay him no more attention because the toppling of the boulder had changed everything. Next to the downed boulder a dark hole was revealed, one that appeared to lead under the sea floor. From it came cooler waters, not heated ones.

Percival grinned with excitement. Two cycles ago, Percy had led Daniel through another hole in the sea floor, through subterranean chasms that were without light but that eventually brought them to a lagoon in the middle of a tropical island. Could this be a similar passageway? The upright, gold-encrusted boulder had been a territorial sign of Pacifica. When it was moved—and Daniel was thrilled that it had been moved by the actions of "Kanonah's pups" assisting the descendants of Saul—the way into Pacifica opened.

Daniel and Percival dashed into the hole, yelling for everyone else to follow. And so, pursued by monsters and not knowing if they would find anything nor even if they would survive, the tribe of Daniel au Fond did at long last enter Pacifica.

10

Paths to the Light

*A*s they traveled farther into the passageway, the light vanished and vision became nearly useless for all those who, like the seals, habitually relied on it. Most of the tribe bumped into the walls on all sides of them, and slowed to make certain they were in the center of the path. Percival, Lavender, and Porphyry passed Daniel. He didn't mind giving up this sort of leadership, for the fluked cousins were better able than pinnipeds to locate by sound and reflected echoes. The seals and sea lions swam eagerly in Porphyry's wake, knowing that if his large body could fit through a passage, they would have no difficulty doing so. Twice Porphyry smashed the sides of the passages, widening them for the horde at his flanks. In the rear of the formation, the leopards guarded against pursuit by the Kratuans.

They paused at a place of several branching passageways, each leading off at an angle. There seemed no reason to choose one instead of another. Nezan shouldered past the stragglers into the leadership. "We want the passage that brings us nearest the surface," Daniel told

Nezan, whose deep, dreaming dives made him sensitive to even the smallest changes in depth and pressure. Near Daniel, little Lokat seemed about to die, and he stared at his grandfather in a plea for help. Daniel had never felt so powerless in his life. "Hurry. The little ones will run out of air."

"This way," Nezan growled, and headed to the left. They coursed through that branch for a hundred lengths, then came to another wide place where channels led off in several directions, each darker than the next. Nezan swung his massive nose from side to side, but could not decide which path to take.

Daniel yearned for better light. There was none. Every other clue to Pacifica had been a pattern. The arrangement of these passageways did remind him of something, but what? Why couldn't his mind just wrap itself around the problem and squeeze until it cracked? The blood pounded in his head as if it would never stop.

Pounding blood! The passageways resembled the pattern of the arteries that carried blood inside a body. The tribe must follow the one that led to the heart. Daniel shouted out his guess, then grasped the back of little Lokat's neck in his teeth and started after the leaders. They immediately began to follow a passageway to the left that seemed more constricted than the others but which soon yielded to another that was wider and slightly brighter, giving Daniel a goal and allowing him to struggle mightily toward the light and a reason not to lose consciousness before he reached air, which he hoped would happen soon or else he would have to burst.

Air! There was air! And light. And land.

They swam in a cavern, the largest Daniel had ever seen, one to match the immense breath that expanded his own chest. He gasped and gasped, though the air was dank and fetid with the scent of sea bottom brought too quickly to the surface. The smell suggested that this vast cave had only recently been opened, perhaps as a result of the biped explosions or the darkening of the sun or the shifting of the gold-encrusted boulder. Globs of mud and stones fell from above. A fire smoldered in a far corner of the cave, where stones that still radiated heat had ignited old wood. Shimmering shadows formed on domed passageways leading off in a half-dozen directions. In the flickering light, brilliant reds and blues and greens leaped from the walls. Many digits of stone tapered down from the cavern's heights, and some reached upward from the banks. Small bubbles stippled the surface of the cave's waters, which stirred with a modest current.

Never had Daniel sensed the great forces so close around him as in this grotto. Elsewhere they were only undercurrents. Here he could almost feel volcanic eruptions and earthquakes. Others—the spirits of sand and ice, the shark of self-doubt, Mandragar the beast of a hundred tentacles, even *Saul, great-great-grandfather of us all*—just seemed to be close about, pounding at the entrance of his mind. The faces of the other whistlers told Daniel that they, too, felt these presences near.

Daniel counted noses. Several were gone. Though little Lokat lay coughing mightily as he rested on Anna, Marlena's and Zelda's most recent pups were nowhere to be seen, and Siwaga had lost two more leopards. The most affected was Popocatepetl, who lay in a shivering ball on a muddy clump, mourning his mate Palenque. Daniel paddled over to Anna, and they nuzzled, grateful for the survival of their immediate family. Lokat, already alert, moved away from them and nosed about the area. A moment later, Anna screamed as Lokat tugged a bone from the muck. It seemed to be part of the rib cage of a sea mammal. Daniel shouldered the pup aside and pulled the bone farther from its resting place. It was connected to others.

"Wenceslas and Esmeralda," Daniel requested, and the walrus and polar bear lumbered to assist. With tusks and claws doing the work, the entire sea-mammal skeleton could soon be seen in the flickering light. But there was no skull. What had happened? Nearby was another skeleton, this one with the elongated leg bones of a biped. Its head, too, was missing.

Now Daniel saw many more things in the high-domed cavern. Half-buried in the mud were toppled and broken statues of stone. It took an examination of a few of these and comparison of shattered parts to determine that they were shaped something like sea lions, with gold pebbles for eyes. They had more pronounced forelimbs and more slender necks than did Daniel's own kind. The creature statues reminded him, Popo, Lavender, and Percival of the crazed beast they had bested in the sargasso, long ago, except that that one had been much larger and had had a long horn imbedded in its forehead.

"The statues are beautiful," Anna said softly.

"But no sea mammal could have made them," Daniel said. "They had to have been fashioned by the more supple digits of bipeds."

"What are the metallic rings about the necks?"

"That, I don't know."

One wall of the cave was partly covered with smooth tiles of the sort Daniel remembered from the floor of the bipeds' laboratory, only these were of many colors and had designs on them. Some tiles had fallen and broken, but it was clear they had once completely covered the wall. Serpents flowed over a series of the tiles; silver teeth gleamed from some others. A giant octopus with nearly countless tentacles was depicted in a third section; it was being attacked by both bipeds and sea lions.

"Mandragar," Daniel whispered. But hadn't old Saul battled this monster with the aid of his bulls? The legend mentioned nothing about bipeds assisting him.

An extensive search and some brushing away of the muck revealed one intact series of tiles. It showed first a sea lion chasing fish in the water, then a pair of sea lions with their heads touching the feet of a biped, then a group of bipeds with fish in their hands. All the eyes were of emerald; the nails on the digits, of turquoise. Some bipeds had hair of gold. What did the series mean?

Daniel stumbled across other tiles—fragments lying in the mud—that were more than puzzling. After looking at one from several angles and sniffing all around, he decided it showed the underside of a sleek-skinned animal being stuck with silver teeth; blood, represented by red agate drops, dripped from the wound. Another showed a pair of biped female legs astride a furred animal with her arms holding kelp lines attached to something in front— Daniel couldn't tell what, or precisely the sort of animal, because the rest of the tile was smashed into many little pieces, scattered about. Looking more closely, he determined that these particular shattered tiles had not fallen from the wall, but had been deliberately torn away and smashed.

"There are other paths," Percy squealed through his eternal grin, as if hoping such paths would yield more pleasant treasures.

In company of Esmeralda, Popo, Lavender, and Nezan—Porphyry could not fit through the smaller passageways—they streaked into lateral openings, and followed these and feeder routes in the stone to discover an entire colony of caverns. Small shafts of light illumined some of these from on high, as if the sun were leaking in from holes in the land far above them. Driftwood, tile, boulders, and shaped stones surrounded pools into which more of the materials had fallen. Clearly, there had once been an entire connected series of grottoes and watery passages, probably at the surface entrance to an island. These had been submerged during the rising of the waters, and later covered over by the shifting of the earth, by lava flows, or by other great natural forces. Some dwelling caves were very beautiful; one, which had come through the cycles mostly intact, was square-shaped and had comfortable resting shelves, decorated above and below and on the walls inside and out with depictions of the sea's bounty. In front of another cave pool was a stunning life-size statue of a sea lion covered with golden metallic fur. Others boasted tile groups of sea lions jumping out of the water and over a golden sun. There were scenes of sea lions and bipeds sharing a feast of crustaceans, of a female biped holding a sea-lion pup in her arms, of a female sea lion suckling a biped pup. An aura swelled through these ruins, something of the sense of glory, majesty, and power, all tinged at the edges with deep sighs of mourning, a feeling Daniel associated with the great triumph of life over the certainty of death.

But there were also grim and ugly things, too, depictions of sea-lion skulls each with a silver ring and silver teeth pointing inward at the neck. An agate sea-lion heart bleeding smaller agates on a solid clamshell of gold. A headless statue that had once been a biped female with a necklace of flipper ends. The statue was intact but for the head, which seemed to have been deliberately removed.

This was Pacifica, but it was not the cove of peace and harmony about which Daniel had hoped and dreamed. It disturbed Daniel greatly. How could this place be the salvation of the world?

Weary with the weight of what he had seen and felt, Daniel followed Percival into another side passageway entirely filled with water that was less briny than that in the grottoes, which was distinctly brackish. Responding to its taste, Percy sent out a series of clicks that even Daniel could hear, and, a moment later, surged forward. Daniel followed his flukes. The darkness yielded steadily to a light coming down toward them in an enormous circle. Percy shot upward, Daniel only a flipper length behind him, the yearning for sunlight like a wave that was thrilling to ride.

Moments later they broke the surface. They were in a lagoon, entirely surrounded by white sands. Even more astounding, a manatee and another recognizable shape, a narwhal, floated in the mostly sweet waters.

"Well, Daniel," said Cendrillon, "it certainly took you long enough to get here."

Part Three

DRIFTWHISTLER

11

Kamarla of Thirteen

"I didn't wait for you in the bay at Silent Turtle Isle, as we had arranged, because there were too many slinky cousins," Cendrillon huffed to Daniel as she chewed her cud at the side of the lagoon and stole a glance at the leopards, who were hauled out on the shores together with the rest of the tribe. Daniel was exhausted, too, but the blubbery manatee with the stumpy front flippers insisted on chattering. "Besides, Fitzwilliam was impatient—you know how these old males are when there's not enough to engage their horns."

"Not quite accurate, my dear," replied the courtly narwhal, waving his spiraled frontal spear aloft. "It was you who regretted the lack of succulent nutrition in the local flora and desired a change of place."

"Ha," the manatee said. "Using the female as an excuse again. Just like you males."

Daniel remembered that Cendrillon had once claimed to have known Saul and Kanonah when they were all young, and that she'd said their disputes were just silly male rivalry. Though Daniel had rejected her claim to great age as improbable, there was no denying she was quite old. So was Fitzwilliam the narwhal, who moved stiffly about the lagoon.

"I regret to point out that the urge to surge was yours," Fitzwilliam said quietly.

"When did you two meet, anyway?" Daniel said, trying to deflect the conversation into calmer waters.

"Three quarters of a moon ago," Fitzwilliam remembered. "Point of Cracked Egg Isle. It was love at first sight."

"A memory as large as a baleen, and as full of empty spaces," sniffed Cendrillon. "It's been two moons now, and it was in the lee of Backbone, and I led him quite a chase before consenting to swim within ten lengths."

"You must agree, at least, on how you knew to come to this place, and how you got into this closed lagoon."

"Any fool could have guessed this location, Daniel," Cendrillon replied. "You needn't have waited for the turtle to come back and die. It's the first land on a direct journey west from Silent Turtle. No trick to it at all."

"Entrance was easy, old chap," Fitzwilliam added. "Long tide spills over that beach, there, once every dozen tides."

"Oh," Daniel said, feeling stupid.

"And did you find Selchie in Pacifica? Such a lovely lassie, as I recall," Cendrillon trilled. "All the males were just crazy about her."

"I don't know what we found, Cendrillon. I'm not sure about anything, after what we saw."

Neither, it seemed, was anyone else. Percival stared at the sun. Porphyry, distracted, rested his massive head on the shore. Lavender hovered five lengths under in the surf, not moving. The entire tribe was disillusioned, a state that added to their physical exhaustion. And the cause, Daniel knew, was Pacifica. What had passed before their eyes in the ruins of Pacifica—the mix of ugliness and beauty—did not resemble the peaceful, cooperative, idealized society of bipeds and sea lions that Daniel had once so lovingly described to the tribe, and that had lured them to Pacifica. Where, in that complex ruin that had so assaulted them, was the promise of a solution to the approaching destruction of the world's oceans?

"Pacifica was a lie, all along," Goshun muttered, and thrashed about the lagoon in rage. "We ought to try to kill all the bipeds, even if we die in the process."

Porphyry sighed as if the sun would not rise in the morning, a sound that was repeated by many around the shores of the lagoon. Porphyry's huge head did not move from its perch—it was as if he wished to beach and die—but then, Daniel thought, he had always had such inclinations. And Goshun's threat that the sea mammals should mount a direct attack upon the bipeds was unrealistic, though it woke in Daniel a pang of memory. Young Goshun's wish to fight to an almost certain death echoed the idea once proposed in a time of crisis by the sea lion for whom Goshun had been named, Tashkent's own father, old Goshun. That was cycles before this young hothead was born. Perhaps bad ideas never settled to sand, but just swirled in the water, generation after generation.

Despair was the underbelly of anger. Daniel could have submerged in such a mindtrap, too, had he not been a prisoner of hope. So many of the ancient legend's conditions had already been fulfilled. The sun had lived in darkness, Kratua had been fought, Kanonah's pups had assisted

Saul's—Daniel wondered if Fred had survived—and Pacifica had been found. There had even been *"storied walls"* in the long-drowned cove. Moreover, his own dream of thirteen tribes acting together, with all of them actually being necessary to pierce through to Pacifica had also been proved correct. Daniel could not have found or entered Pacifica without the help of such brothers and sisters as Porphyry, Percival, Popocatepetl, Esmeralda, Nezan, and Lavender. One task remained: to seize the *"gold of understanding."*

"As soon as we're rested and have regained our strength," he announced, "we must go back into Pacifica."

"No." "Never." "Let's get out of here." The shouts arose from all places in and around the lagoon.

"If we don't go in, the terrible things that are happening will get worse—the waste, the ooze, the fish die-offs, the killing red tides! Remember the verse:

"But should the tide pool still not clear,
The very oceans shall disappear."

"Who cares? If we're going to die, I don't want it to be in that awful cave," Marlena piped up.

"Soon as long tide comes, I'm outta here," said young Glex.

"Then what will you do if you come upon the ooze again?"

"We'll swim around it, even if that means a detour of ten thousand lengths," said Filomena.

"We can't save the world, Daniel," Goshun shouted. "We may not even be able to save ourselves." Heads nodded sagely agreement with the young bull. "Pacifica shows how terrible the bipeds have been to us since the days of our forefathers. They maim. They kill. They spew their waste all over our territories. They always have, and they always will. Now that we know it for certain, we'll spend our lives staying away from them, and if they corner us, well, then, we'll know that to give up is to endure tremendous pain, and so we'll never give up, but swim and fight and kill as many of them as we can before we go to sand."

The nodding heads were grim and closemouthed. The majority of the tribe agreed with Goshun.

The path ahead became obvious to Daniel.

"If that's the way you feel about it, Goshun," he began, "then you can lead the tribe, and take everyone with you when you go."

There was a murmur of amazement. Would Daniel give up the leadership so easily, without a real fight? Daniel hoped his sudden announcement would stun the swimmers into listening more closely.

"You're not quite a beachmaster yet, Goshun, but you will be, I've no doubt about that, and those who follow you will be able to do so with confidence. Not me. I'm older and grayer now, Goshun, and I've slowed down a lot. It's not just this flipper wound that won't heal, it's everything. I've reached a point where leadership doesn't mean as much to me, now, as some other matters—like understanding the world, and accepting my proper place in the grand cycle of life and death. If I don't make sense out of Pacifica, my life is finished, my son. It's taken a long time to realize that, but now I know what to do. I'm going to stay here and, as soon as I can, dive back into Pacifica and do my best to figure out its mysteries. Any who wish to stay with me are welcome—I need all the help I can get—but I won't command any of you to stay."

There could be no mass leaving for several tides more, since the way to the sea was still filled with sand, but it seemed likely that most of the tribe would go, under the leadership of Goshun, who loped about, trying to appear beachmasterly. Anna would stay, Daniel was glad to hear, and so would the whistlers, including Cendrillon.

It was the old sea cow who suggested that since they had to wait, and since they had actually been fasting for some time because of the lack of proper food in the lagoon and the long subterranean journey the tribe had made, they might as well pass the time by having a kamarla.

"A kamarla of all thirteen tribes!" Daniel exclaimed. "I've been wanting that for cycles. There hasn't been one since—actually, we don't even know when there was one before this time, if there ever was."

The other whistlers seemed eager for a kamarla, to the point where Daniel wondered if they'd been waiting for just such an opportunity. Kamarlas were rather pleasant, which accounted for the suggestion receiving no resistance from the tribal members who had decided to go with Goshun.

The kamarla started slowly, with some moments of quiet observation of the sun being eaten by the sea. Daniel had never taken part in the old ceremony with as much fervor as he did during these waves, but he was silent, as were the others who would otherwise have intoned the verses celebrating this event, so as not to offend those who no longer believed in it. Then the many sorts of animals who made up the tribe overlapped their bodies, some entirely in the lagoon, most situated on the shore with hindquarters in the water. The narwhal lay down with the leopards, the elephant with the tiny otter, the baleen with the dolphin, all sorts and ages and genders of seals and sea lions nestled together, eyes closed, and, under the gentle urgings of the whistlers' chants, let their minds intermingle as fully as their strong scents. They were thirteen tribes, thirteen descendants of Beachmaster Saul, brought together in the vicinity of Pacifica. They were many and they were one, a mass of sea mammals in whom lay the hope of the world.

The warmth of the bodies, the gentle sound of the surf, the beauty of the dark night, the repetitive sounds intoned by the whistlers, all produced in Daniel a sense of kinship, a feeling of power beyond that of his own mind and body. He felt an infusion of strength and certainty, as if the tribe were willing its senses and mind into his own. He became completely convinced that despite the assistance of the others that he had received before this moment, it was now his task alone to rescue the legend from the horror of the caverns. The whistlers were not the answer; he was the potential driftwhistler.

Daniel felt teeth and flippers and fins grab at him. It was pleasant, at first, a sort of massage accompanied by increasingly insistent chants from the whistlers. He had a moment of brief panic when he opened his eyes for a moment and caught sight of Fitzwilliam's horn being rubbed against him, but soon felt an almost irresistible urge to sleep. But what were the black leaves impaled on the narwhal's spear? Could they be nightbloods? They'd kill him! Daniel struggled to move and discovered he could not do so, that his limbs would not respond.

He felt himself being pushed beneath the surface by Percival and Esme and the other whistlers. They'd drown him! Without conscious thought, his membranes closed his nostrils and lungs to air. He was helpless, carried along by those who were supposed to be his friends, going down, down, into the darkness of the Pacifican caverns. As his body was forced into the darkness, he felt his mind similarly growing empty of all thoughts of the surface. He was struggling against death, but with what weapons?

He could no longer see. He wanted to open his eyes, but there was nothing, not even flashes of light. He opened his mouth to scream, but had no voice. Yet he sensed things. The journey had stopped, and he was at rest; the other bodies and flippers no longer touched his, but did not truly leave him alone. He was thirteen tribes. He was powerful with their minds.

"You will enter the drowned world," a thunderous voice sounded in his ear. "You will battle the shades of Pacifica. You will solve the terrible mysteries, or you will not return to life. You are the driftwhistler."

12

Pacifica Dreams

*A*s in a storm, the sea and sky became one and there was no distinction between above and below the surface. Daniel's mind reached out for his companions, but could not find them, though he held their wisdom in his own. A single animal, he struggled toward what seemed a shore of white light that shafted at him in bursts of energy. Was this real, a dream, or something else? Daniel could not tell, but neither could he escape being in Pacifica. Shadows leaked into the light and became recognizable as the threatening undulations of a black manta ray about to cross his path. He snarled at the enemy. Unexpectedly, it exploded to fish that glided underneath him, but that he could not grasp. A play of light and dark dappled an upright boulder with the shapes of sea lions on it; their golden eyes winked at him.

He reclined on a stone perch in a cavern of great beauty. Daniel glanced down at his body and was disturbed to see that it was of a golden color, larger than he was used to, and that his forelimbs were longer. Who was he? A rounded young female swam by him; he followed her with his eyes until she vanished. There were others in the cavern now, many companions, male and female, animal and biped. Bipeds! But they didn't resemble the bipeds Daniel had known; they were smaller and had deeper-set eyes. They seemed to hold him in high regard; they bent their necks to him, offered to satisfy his every want. He was not only dominant, he was the object of their love.

The pleasant sensation of reclining in the cavern did not last. Daniel blinked his eyes and he and his companions were swimming together along narrow grottoes and then out into the sunlit expanses of tropical ocean. Waves like heartbeats of cloud hurled toward the shore, and Daniel raced along their edges. A biped surfed alongside him. He loved this biped. On the curl of surf, as if aboard a lightning bolt, they rode and sang, the biped friend holding a music maker of wood and sinews; they made noise as joyful as raindrops.

Something was falling, drop by drop, into a tide pool about his foreflippers. He was in the cave of the sun's death agony, and himself about to die. He yearned for one more tomorrow, but thought he would never see it. The sand monster lurked beneath the belly of his mind, always hungry, blasting at everything he had ever known, birthing intense doubts. The cold north wind at his flanks sought with its tentacles to freeze his thoughts to the pace of snails. He turned to get at his tormentors, and they stayed just out of touch, dancing in the firelight that played on the walls.

What was going on? Who was he? At one moment he felt like Saul, but at another he was in some different life. Everything was jumbled up together, and he did not know if he could sort it out.

He dreamed of the female who had swum by, and she approached again, her limpid eyes now in shadow, now with the quality of stars. She was two, four, a dozen females, a harem of illusions. She was the freezing north wind, the biting, swirling sands. Was she his love, or his death? Daniel couldn't be sure. He shook himself to clear his head, but it would not clear. He was in the past—that much he knew—but where? Was he Saul? Was this female with the tide-pool eyes Selchie? Emotions rushed through his mind. He was a participant in the feast, yet he was to be eaten; he was sea lion and yet not sea lion; he was beyond mortal, yet about to die.

How could he be all these things? Reason and direction must explain the confusing torrent of images. He must separate the strands. He could not have been all of these things at once. Monsters of sand and cold wind hovered near, but Daniel, trained by whistlers, knew now how to keep great forces from the killing blow. He sank into the nightbloods, let their powerful poison form a shield against the monsters. But in the nightbloods' grasp he had to continue to search, for if he relaxed the poison would submerge him forever. He let his every impulse embrace its opposite until the ripples in the tide pool stilled.

Clearer, now. There were two lives whose auras he felt, one that was Saul and another that had lived earlier, a being that did not have a name, a being who sat on a high perch, everything and everyone below him. Daniel's golden coat seemed more dolphinlike than a sea lion's covering, and he had forequarters more pronounced than a sea lion's. He was content: groomed, sated, warm, fulfilled, confident. Off to his left flipper, a bevy of females awaited him, willing partners. By his other flipper, shallow pools of fish swam, ready to satisfy his appetite for food. Sun filled the day, invigorating surf kissed the beaches below, and just enough clouds on the horizon relieved the monotony of the perfectly blue sky. He was supreme among all the animals of the world. Bipeds approached him warily to place flowers between his flippers, to bow and kneel, to gaze at him. Their voices sang his praises; their clothing showed likenesses of him, and the icons they bore resembled him, small statues whose eyes and fur were of gold. His shape was everywhere: on boulders, on tiles, even in the contours of passageways through the rocks and in outlines drawn on the sea floor. Should he desire exercise, other animals would clear a path for him, beat back enemies, and assure that his route to the sea would be filled with beautiful corals and other wondrous sights. Just then he was desirous of nothing but to bask in the sunlight of his own magnificence. His life was satisfaction. In the prime of life, he felt he would never yield his beachmastership.

One biped in the cavern showed distaste at his animal smell. He waved a flipper, and at his command bipeds did his bidding and killed the disbeliever. The dead biped lay in the pool. He waved his other flipper to have the body taken away, and decided to have a celebration, a feast of love, of song, of food. All the seagoing animals were happy, swimming, eating, coupling, joining their voices in song. He desired a female and summoned a lovely young cow onto his series of perches. She was too fearful of his magnificence for conversation, but she was compliant. When the sky darkened to night, the bipeds built fires to keep them warm and to provide light. Unusual delicacies and flowers were brought to fuel the celebrations. Inside a circle of bipeds, the seagoing animals honored him as their leader.

His life was perfect. When the sand monster attacked, he swiped at it with a thousand teeth and shattered the sand into countless bits that the tide took away—all but one bit, a mote in his eye, a slight sense of loneliness. All the animals, male and female, deferred to him and no one challenged his thoughts or desires. That was worrisome. His loneliness increased. Fewer and fewer animals rimmed his gold-encrusted pool, but there were more bipeds near, bringing him what he needed and desired. The bipeds wanted him constantly with them. This was a new sensation, adoration by the bipeds, who fed him, groomed him, sang to him alone. They stroked his fur, and some of the biped females embraced him repeatedly. He hardly felt like an animal any longer, for an animal needed others of his kind, and he had none; he was the object of the bipeds' admiration, though, and had to take comfort from that.

The male bipeds honored him by inviting him aboard a floater. They knew how he liked the wind ruffling his fur, and took him for a sail over the waters in a floater aimed toward another island. His warriors, bipeds with the image of himself on kelp strips bound about their heads, screamed intense anger and desire at the other island. Reaching the shallows, he leaped out of the floater and led them into battle against other bipeds. His warriors took strength from his beauty and power.

Vanquished, the bipeds of the second island were

brought back to be slaves to his own bipeds. At a celebration of victory he was honored even more. They gave him special bowls from which to drink. The liquid was delicious. Male and female slave bipeds groomed his fur. Dusk came, and they sang to him, but when night arrived, they lit no fires, just continued to groom him, murmur pleasant sounds, and offer more to drink. The darkness of the night intensified. Immobile and anxious, he awaited the dawn.

With first light, more bipeds entered his tide pool, where the image of him gleamed from the tiles on the floor. They approached him as they had done so many times when they had brought flowers, but this time their hands bore silver teeth. Males and females came nearer and nearer. They sang to him, praised him, surrounded him. There was no escape. He could not move. Silver teeth bit into him from many directions. He shuddered with their attacks, though, strangely, he felt no pain, as if the bites were those of bats. Drops and streams of his blood reddened the tide pool. Dawn was breaking over the island, but night spread through his mind; his aura flew out of him as he rushed to embrace his own blood and died.

The darkness comforted, the warmth nurtured, the current lulled. Then it rocked, and sent him again on the journey through passageways whose sides pressed in on him until he was ready to scream.

He reached the sunlight and was alive again, but different from before. His coat was more like fur, his forelimbs shorter and more like flippers. He had a name, now, and that name was Saul. Daniel let his mind sink into Saul. In contrast to the former life, Saul's was vigorous but at peace, secure because he knew the course of his days and nights. He had many satisfying constants: the daily transit of the sun, the cycles of the moon, the waves lapping at the shore, the excitement of the hunt, his love for his master. He understood that he coursed between birth and death on a known current.

But just as a yearning to see tomorrow's sun informs the night, a thought nibbled at Saul's mind, a desire for something unnamed, a hunger that had not been sated. This yearning occupied only a shadowed corner of the cave of his mind, but he knew it was there.

When Saul was younger, the iron ring about his neck had not made its presence felt so keenly, and he had not been as hungry. When he and Kanonah had first learned to hunt together, he had been able to swallow as many fish as he could snap up. No longer. Now the ring prevented him from swallowing fish in a bite or two. He ate only after he had delivered to Kanonah all the fish he could catch in a tide. Then the master would kindly cut a few fish into very small bits that he could chew down without difficulty. The master was good to him in such ways. He would never leave Kanonah, for such an attempt would result in slow starvation; an animal alone cannot feed himself properly, the elders advised.

Besides, Saul loved Kanonah, and they had wonderful times together, racing out in the open sea, shooting the curl of the surf, or, with Kanonah hanging on to kelp lines attached to Saul's ring, gliding down to the bottom where they would search for pearls in oysters. Of course, they had both been younger then, and the master had not had so many responsibilities. But Saul kept that moment always in his mind as the essence of happiness, of enjoying life together, sea lion and biped.

Older and wiser now, he was fortunate in not having to perform the tasks that were the lot of many of the other animals. Those were seagoers too, he supposed, but generations of breeding had made them different from him, fit only for dull tasks such as hauling up gold-bearing rocks from great depths, or propelling rock-laden floaters through currents and surf into the cove of grottoes. He didn't like those hauler animals. He also disdained the slippery finned ones who were used to send messages to other islands and who never had to do a day's fishing, though they wore rings as he did. And he hated the lumbering, stupid, slow-flippered bulls of enormous size and strength. Yes, he was grateful to Kanonah for the opportunity he gave, now and then, to fight one of these ugly beasts.

On great occasions the bipeds and their animals would gather at the edges of the gold-rimmed killing pool for the contests. Saul felt an affinity for that place that had the image of the golden forebear in the tiles at the pool's bottom. When he entered this pool, he always felt it was the proper place for him to be. Amidst shouts and feasting, he could demonstrate his bravery, his strength and skills, and the firmness of his love for the master. Five times, in the killing pool, he had fought to the finish. No bowing of the neck by the loser to the victor in these contests. Death to the vanquished! It was a chance to strike a blow to honor one's master.

Blows came at him faster than he could resist, this time, from slashing teeth of great sharpness and shoulder rams of awesome strength. He weaved, slid, scrambled, and tried to turn and slice at his opponent's flipper, but the big bull was too much for him, a bull with a body like a boulder and flippers able to launch a near tidal wave. Saul twisted and strained to evade the thrusts. His breath came in short gasps. If he did not avoid the blows, he would die.

Across the killing pool, he caught a glimpse of a slim female sea lion leaping into the pool, her mistress shouting alarm after her but not daring to go in and grab her ring for fear of the clashing bulls. His opponent was distracted by the beauty, and in that moment Saul sprang with all his might for the bull's neck, concentrating his force on pressing the ring inward so that it choked. Blood poured from the bull's mouth and the bull died.

Cold. Inability to savor the victory. The north wind and the sand-monster hovered at his flanks. He wanted to lie very still. When the sun dispelled the shadows, Kanonah went to fish and left him alone to sleep in the tide pool of their cave.

Selchie peered at him with her soft brown eyes. How had she found him, lying near death on this dry perch? He wanted to thank her for distracting the bull, but he was too weak. He lay back and gloried in the songs of the moon she sang and in the way she warmed the flipper that had grown so cold. The sun passed through the sky several times, and he knew no constant except her. Selchie's mistress was not aware that she was loose, that her ring had rusted at its connection to the chain. Though she had to arrange the chain so that it appeared she had never left, and return to her home cave before dusk, Selchie had the run of the grottoes in the days. For the first time, Saul felt love for someone other than the master. As the pod of floaters led by Kanonah approached, they would hear it; Selchie would nuzzle him and then flee the cave to return to her own.

As her visits continued, Saul gained strength and joy, but hid both from Kanonah, from whom he had never before concealed anything. The love he felt for Selchie filled him so that he had no desire for the fish liquid Kanonah offered him in the evenings. As he ate less and less, the ring loosened its hold on his neck. He further compromised the ring by thumping and cracking its old metal against the stones at the side of the pool. These matters, too, he concealed from the master, at first in great terror at withholding anything from the biped who had trained him; later he hid the cracked ring with fierce delight.

The sun was up and Selchie had not come. Kanonah beat him with hands and feet, lashed at him with strands of wood and skin, shouted anger and reproach. Why? He was only refusing to go to sea this one day, suffused with longing for his cow. Where was she? What had the bipeds done with her? *To* her? Kanonah's voice told him he was bad, was wrong, was low. The blows he could endure, had suffered them before, but not the reproachful voice of his friend and companion telling him that he deserved punishment. For what? For being who he was, a sea lion? He weaved, twisted, thrust to get away from the awful voice of hate, but it would not stop. He must stop it, must make the master understand that it was only he, Saul, acting as a sea lion, and that he must have love.

The chain swung at the master's mouth, knocking him back and away and into silence. But how could the chain do that unless it no longer held! Broken halves of the ring from Saul's neck sank toward the tiles of the pool's bottom. Blood leaked down as well, but he did not feel its loss because he was free.

Searching for Selchie among the grottoes, sniffing, looking, touching everywhere during the darkest of tides while the bipeds slept: He was his senses. Each pool was home to a bull or a cow, each animal kept apart from the others, chained to a master's wall. These haulers and float pullers and rock bearers and message carriers were not his enemies, as the biped masters had insisted in the killing pool; they were more like him than he was like the bipeds. Saul saw these bulls now and did not hate them.

He dripped his red fire into the pools of his brothers and they ate the drops and knew courage, became enraged and certain and powerful enough to break their chains and follow his search.

Rip, smash, jar, tear, slash, rake: His bulls were anger, were motion, were light. Behead the boulder! Crack the tile! Smear it all in mud and filth! Death to the walls, the grottoes, the shelves, the biped masters whose love was only chains, whose kindness was only the absence of pain.

Saul and his bulls fought the bipeds, then, fin and flipper against hand. Many died on both sides, but the bipeds could not contain the swimmers. They were slaves no more. They had no masters. And Saul was their leader; he was the night that erased the day; he was the sea, fluid, supple, impossible to deny. His rage was joined by the

north wind that cut like ice, the sand that smashed everything to bits of itself. They were one with him, and they
would obliterate the land and its bipeds.

He and the bulls searched for Selchie amid the defiled
caverns, and found her, high in a grotto, held against a
wall by Kanonah, who had many silver teeth. Kanonah
would release her if Saul came near enough to be captured.
Saul hesitated. The bulls told him he could not save her
and himself. He crawled closer to the biped. Kanonah
thrust at him with a silver tooth, and Selchie shouted at
him to go. He hesitated. He could neither go nor approach
the biped. There was a roaring in his head, a roaring born
of his dilemma. How could he save his love and save his
own life? The roaring grew louder and louder—and the
other bulls heard it, too, and so did Kanonah and Selchie,
a belching, screeching, grumbling noise that toppled
shelves and perches, caused boulders to fly loose. It was
the land! The land itself had joined the sea, the north wind,
and the sand in anger at the bipeds. The caverns shook
and began to collapse. He shouted to Selchie to come with
him but she could not, because she was unable to free
herself from Kanonah.

She shouted at him to go, and at last he had no choice
but to save himself. The bulls, and the few cows that were
able to, swam away as the island breathed fire and spewed
black ash to the sky. The blackness spread across the sky
like night, shading the sun's face, then darkening it, then
obscuring it. The ash began to waft down, black petals,
drifting toward the sea, pieces of night, black drops, the
petals of the nightblood. Rain began, washing the black-

ness before it into the great waters of the sea, the cleansing waters, the never-still waters, the waters of life.

~~~~~

Daniel awoke on the shore of the lagoon as water was splashed gently on his face. He was not Saul, he was not the unknown forebear, he was himself, Daniel au Fond. It was wonderful to be alone with your own mind, not to have to bear the burden of so many others. He was so exhausted that he could hardly move, yet he felt completely at peace with the sea, the sky, and all the friendly faces that peered so lovingly at his own.

13

~~~~~~

Driftwhistler

"What did you see?" the whistlers and everyone else in the tribe wanted to know.

Daniel did not immediately answer. He made as an excuse for silence the need to clear his mind from the lingering effects of the nightbloods and his journey, but that was not the problem. His difficulty lay in how to relate what he had experienced in the caverns of Pacifica. Seeing the anxious expressions on the whistlers' faces, he knew he had traveled beyond any of their journeys in the spirit world. While they had occasionally wrestled with the north wind and the bottom sands, he had known these forces as constant companions. Could he explain to the tribe the astounding things he had seen? And what of the tribe's prior conception of Pacifica, the one he had formerly shared, the one his explanation would surely shatter? What was his real responsibility to the tribe? To the whistlers? To the past in whose belly he had lain? To the future?

For a tide, he weighed these questions. He rested alongside Anna, felt her warmth, her unconditional acceptance of him, her steady belief that their love would endure and prevail. None of the animals, not even the whistlers, had known what sort of creature a driftwhistler might be. As he rested beside Anna, Daniel came to the realization that the driftwhistler was more than one who felt keenly those natural forces of the world that swirled around all beings but whose effects most animals did not acknowledge. To be a driftwhistler was to create legends. Saul had been the first driftwhistler—that was now obvious, because what the legend said about Pacifica was not precisely what had happened in Pacifica. Saul had interpreted the past to provide direction and inspiration to those who escaped with him. Now that Pacifica had been regained, it was up to Daniel to invent a legend that would inspire the future.

So it was that Daniel au Fond began to tell to the assembled members of thirteen tribes a tale that he hoped would be of vibrant and immediate use. First, he sang two of the old verses:

"In Pacifica all sing the melody of pearl,
The gold of understanding, all whirl
In endless dance 'neath sun and wave:
All hail Pacifica, cove of the brave.

"In Pacifica did lions and bipeds thrive,
Nor could one without the other live,
Biped and sea lion, hand and flipper,
Linked in the jaws of forever."

Heads nodded at these old and familiar words, but stopped moving when Daniel suggested that these verses did not mean what had always been supposed, did not say that Pacifica was an idyllic cove in which bipeds and sea lions enjoyed a harmonious, love-filled existence.

"We believed harmony had to be joyous," he told the tribe. "That's why we were all so shocked to see the likenesses of sea lions in rings and chains, the broken and fouled tiles, the evidence of so many beheadings and other killings and bloodlettings. We believed in the harmony of working together, as we did on our long journey to find and enter Pacifica. But in the old days harmony was simply an order imposed by the powerful. Each couldn't exist without the other, all right, but the linkage wasn't really good—wasn't true cooperation."

The faces of Percival and Esmeralda set hard, as if carved out of stone. Seeing the changes in their usual grins, Daniel knew he was on the right path, for he understood that the whistlers had guessed and feared as much. As the tides came and went, he spoke of two eras. The harmony of the first was false, he said, because sea animals had been set up as perfect creatures, and homage had been paid to them by the bipeds. He could not precisely call the golden-furred creature in whose mind he had temporarily lived a sea lion, because he had seemed more ancient than that. Homage from the bipeds had lasted only as long as the golden creature was useful, he pointed out. When there was something to celebrate, the bipeds killed the golden one to whom they had earlier bent their necks in submission.

"Usually the golden creature was appealed to by the bipeds as we appeal to Saul in the stars," Daniel said to the listening tribes, "but they killed him when they felt like it, sometimes for no reason at all. So the celebration of sea lions wasn't true harmony." Daniel told the story of the golden one's life in great detail. What veneration the old forebear had received! Yet Daniel let the tribe know that the forebear through whose eyes he had experienced the period of adulation was an animal deluded into having no sense of the killing-pool death that so clearly awaited him. No, sea lions were not to be appealed to as stars or set up as superior to any other animals or species. Sea lions were a part of their world, no more, no less.

When this had sunk into the minds of his listeners, Daniel then began on the story of Saul the slave.

"A slave?" Goshun asked, incredulous.

"No more, no less," Daniel nodded. He detailed the arrangements for the sea lions of that era, each in separate pools, each held by a biped family. He spoke of the chains, the rings, of adult animals growing into the rings to the point where they could no longer swallow their food normally, of the system for producing new sea lions and binding them with love to their biped masters instead of to their actual fathers and mothers. He showed them how this love had been twisted to allow the bipeds to control adult animals and make them do tasks for the benefit of the bipeds alone.

It was as if the north wind had settled on his listeners' shoulders: They were chilled to silence. He related the tasks of the animals of Pacifica: the messenger work, the scouting, the hunting, the gathering of pearls, the hauling up of gold-bearing rocks, the pulling of loaded floaters. Though he despised the period of domination by the bipeds, Daniel spoke kindly of the early relationship between the master named Kanonah and his slave sea lion named Saul.

There had been wonderful moments when they had ridden the surf together, man and animal both enjoying the wind and the power of the sea, shooting along the curl of a wave on a day of bright sunlight. If there had been any true harmony in Pacifica, it had been at such moments— and such moments had been thrilling. But, Daniel insisted grimly, they had not lasted.

Daniel then related the uprising that brought an end to biped domination—indeed, an end to Pacifica. He was careful to mention, and actually to embellish, the role of each of the sea mammal tribes, and to state that the breaking of the domination of the bipeds could not have been accomplished but for the strength of the hauler walrus, the fleetness of the messenger dolphin, the courage of the fisher leopard seal, and so on.

"You mean we're not all sons of Saul?" Nezan asked, incredulous.

"We have an even closer relationship," Daniel replied. "Saul and the other animals were brothers under the skin."

The uprising was a triumph for the sea mammals, Daniel went on, but not without its cost. The sea lions who rid themselves of their chains also let loose their anger on the innocent as well as on the dominators, and that was terrible. This Daniel symbolized by the story of Selchie.

"Yes, there was a real cow by that name, as beautiful as any of those here now, the equal of my gracious Anna, and as full of compassion. Selchie helped Saul in his time of need, and when Kanonah held her hostage to make Saul stay, she would not encourage the man and sea lion to fight, and would not allow the enraged animals to kill the biped, either. It was Selchie who prevented them from destroying everything out of their own anger. She was indeed the mother of us all—but not in the way the old legend said. The story of Kanonah stealing Selchie was an invention of Saul's that came out of his anger at the master for what had happened and his sorrow at having left her behind. Even more than Saul, Selchie saw that Kanonah cared for the sea lions but was caught up in a system based on hate."

In the escape, Daniel continued, Saul and his brother animals were aided by the great forces of the spirit world, the north wind and the sand bottom, those creatures whom the whistlers always invoked. Saul and the animals had been of equal power to these great forces, because the animals *were* the sea. During the escape, all the great forces acted as one, and not even the once-dominant bipeds could withstand their power. The land rejected the hate-filled cove that Pacifica had become, and the eruption sank it beneath the waters, to wait for countless cycles until Daniel and his tribe had finally come to seek their source.

~~~~

After Daniel finished with his story of escape, his listeners were all distraught, and he felt a bit sad. But Daniel was convinced that every individual sea mammal must make his or her own peace with the central fact underlying the tale: that the joyous harmony of the place of their dreams had never really existed. A continued belief in the mythical Pacifica of the past—and a yearning to return somehow to the supposedly wonderful days of long ago—

would continue to hinder believers from dealing properly with the problems of the present. You could not swim in the same waters twice.

The present was his main focus, the reason he presumed to become driftwhistler to this tale. In the telling, he hoped to give his listeners the courage to face the current problems of the world, and an understanding that could lead to a better future.

"The oceans are still in danger of dying," Daniel began again. "And we must do something about it, use what we have gained from learning what went wrong in Pacifica. We now know the answer to the puzzle of why the bipeds exploit the seas, try to kill off the seagoing races, and dump their garbage into the seas. It's because bipeds still think of us as slaves! Everything bad that has happened to the oceans since the time of Pacifica has come about because the bipeds have not yet ceased to think of themselves as masters, and of all other beings as inferior to them."

"That's true," a cow said. A second nodded agreement and another took up the cry until heads were bobbing in assent all over the lagoon.

"I say attack 'em," Wenceslas growled, and a half-dozen other large bulls grunted in agreement. "Kill the bipeds!"

"What good would that do?" asked Daniel.

"We'd be the masters," the walrus responded.

"The task of the former slave is never to become a master," Daniel shouted, "but to make sure that there are no slaves anywhere."

"How could we do that?" Goshun roared, just as loudly. "Let's avoid the bipeds—go off by ourselves, somewhere, and stay away from them. We'll find and make a new Pacifica. One that doesn't have any bipeds."

"That's no longer possible," Daniel answered calmly. "Bipeds are everywhere."

"Then what shall we do, my flippered friend?" Percival piped up.

"Yes, what shall we do?" Esmeralda echoed.

"We must make the bipeds stop treating us as inferior beings."

"Not very likely, Daniel," Goshun said. "They've been harsh to sea mammals since—since Pacifica. The cruelty that was born in Pacifica has been the basis for the way they've dealt with sea mammals all these cycles. Your experiences just proved that."

"Not all bipeds are cruel. And even some who become cruel may once have wanted to ride the surf with us! And I think they still want to do so."

"How do you know?"

"I don't know. But I want the bipeds to understand and accept us as equals."

"They'll never do that," Goshun objected.

"How can you be sure?" Daniel confronted him. "How can we ever make progress unless we try to convince them to treat us fairly?"

"It just doesn't seem possible, Daniel. We don't speak their language, they're used to cruelty, they like to torture us, and . . . and . . . and—"

"You're just saying that, my son, because *you* were badly treated once. I want you to be generous about your captors and not full of anger. The task of the former slave is to rise above bad treatment."

"Why? Why not just swim away from them all?"

"Kanonah once treated Saul as an equal," Daniel insisted.

"Yes, but he didn't do it for very long."

The argument between Daniel and Goshun went on for almost a tide, through the night, and would not resolve. In the old way of doing things, Daniel and Goshun would have fought it out physically, and the bull who survived would impose his way on the tribe. But in the aftermath of his journey into the heart of Pacifica, Daniel refused to come to blows, and Goshun seemed to have grown up enough not to insist on a fight.

Goshun told in detail what had happened to him when he had been taken away from Silent Turtle Isle by the airfloater. He had been made to perform tricks like balancing a toy on his nose and jumping through hoops in the water, and he had been punished and starved when he didn't do those things. Though no spiked ring had been placed around his growing neck, he had been just as much a slave as old Saul. And had been more humiliated by being forced to do things that no sea lion normally did.

"But you are stronger for having survived the ordeal," Daniel countered. "You have a strength that no one can ever take away from you, a strength that comes from seeing and experiencing the worst, and knowing that you are better than bad treatment."

Goshun accepted that he did have this strength, but would not be shaken from his belief that bipeds were to be avoided. Daniel told Goshun what he had in mind to do, and Goshun appreciated the task, but said he would prefer not to participate in it because he could not do so wholeheartedly.

And so they did not fight, but agreed to disagree. As Daniel's experience had been different from Tashkent's, and Tashkent's from his own father's, so Goshun's differed from Daniel's own—but it did not cause Goshun and Daniel to be enemies. They were not entirely friends, but were linked in the blood in an even stronger way that allowed them to respect their differences. They did agree to a new division of the leadership.

"It's your time, son," Daniel said, "and I have another task to do."

"I'll make sure that the tribe is safe, and that we get away from this place."

"If you're leading them, I'll breathe easier."

"I'll take care of it."

The first swells of the leap tide began to reach over the white sands that separated the lagoon from the ocean. It was a brilliant, breeze-filled day, with white clouds celebrating the pure blue of the sky. Before the sun moved much higher in the sky, the passage to the sea would be open.

Daniel looked down into the lagoon, and what peered back at him was an old bull, almost a whitefur as his grandfather, Goshun, and father, Tashkent, had become as they aged. He didn't feel old, but he would never be able to swim as swiftly on that hurt flipper, and as he watched the pups and youngsters scamper about, bored with the talk of the adults, he felt a growing distance from their concerns. Their minds were filled with thoughts of food, of play, of mating, matters that were less important to him now than the sweep of the cycles, the interweaving of nature's forces, the need for harmony between sea and land. To be a driftwhistler was not to earn a title but to speak with a certain power, a power that brought with it great responsibilities. The driftwhistler touches what his listeners already know, what they already feel in their hearts and have not had the courage to embrace. And that puts both speaker and listener at great risk.

Gaining the tribe's attention again, Daniel announced that he was willingly ceding the beachmastership permanently to Goshun, and that the sojourn of the tribe in the waters of Pacifica was coming to an end.

"Those who wish to go home, or elsewhere on the oceans, you have my thanks and my good wishes," Daniel told his former charges. "Goshun will lead you away from here. You will go forth, I hope, with a new understanding of Pacifica. You know now what sea mammals have only guessed at in the past: that we are free, but that nothing of great worth in this world can be accomplished without the aid of others."

There was general agreement on that point. Various groups indicated their willingness to leave as soon as the leap tide was full. Siwaga's leopards didn't like the hot climate and wanted to return home; the red-brown seal Glex and the walrus Wenceslas would travel with them to the southern archipelago. The northern dappled seals also yearned for their ice-filled climate, and the otter Popocatepetl wished to travel with them; he was lonely and wanted to find a new mate. Goshun would lead them to the edge of the continent, and then groups would diverge north and south.

"But I'm staying here," Daniel told them. "I have a task to do."

"What's that?" Percival quickly asked.

"You know what it is, Percy. And so do the rest of you who've put your minds to thinking about Pacifica and the legend. We must try to ride the surf with the most difficult of companions."

Anna moved to his side. "Are we really going to do it?" she asked.

"Yes." He nuzzled her fondly. "You are more of a daughter of Selchie than I knew. I couldn't have understood her without you."

"Flattery will get you anywhere," Anna grinned.

Little Lokat gazed up at him steadily and tried not to look at his mother, Filomena, and father, Goshun, who were to leave without him. Lokat would be his apprentice, Daniel thought to himself.

"It won't be easy, Daniel," Esmeralda pointed out.

"If it were easy, it would have been accomplished long ago," Lavender responded. "Let's do it, Daniel."

"Do you need any ugly old grandmothers in your group?" said Cendrillon, swaying her hindquarters in the first wash of the leap tide.

"I'm uglier than you are," Nezan the elephant seal pointed out, "and I'm staying."

"We need as many different tribes as we can muster," Daniel said.

"If you'll help me over the beach, I'll stay with you and teach," Porphyry sighed.

They all pushed and shoved Porphyry as the leap tide crested and waves lapped over the sands to the edge of the lagoon, enabling them to get the big baleen moving. The tribe began to swim away from the barren island, past the curl of the incoming surf, out to deeper waters.

Just past the surf point, the two groups said their farewells. Goshun and many others, including the leopards, Filomena and her clan of northerners, Marlena and Esther and some old sea lions shepherding the younger generation, flanked by the bulls Wenceslas, Glex, and Popocatepetl, started off toward the east. Daniel, Anna, little Lokat, Nezan and Parduk, Cendrillon and Fitzwilliam, Percival, Lavender, Esmeralda, and Porphyry huddled together and said their good-byes to the others.

"Will we ever see them again?" Anna wondered.

"Though the seas are vast, the paths of the exceptional are remarkably intertwined," Percival laughed.

"You and your old dolphinic sayings," Daniel laughed at him. Then, with his heart in his mouth, he turned toward the beach of the central island, on which was sited the colony of bipeds that included Fred and those who had watched the sun live that one terrible and wonderful day in darkness.

"Are you ready, Lokat?"

"Yes, Grampa," the little one replied, and practiced the motion Daniel had showed him, the biped flipper signal of greeting that Fred had taught Daniel cycles ago in the biped laboratory.

Once on the beach, Daniel planned for the strange collection of sea mammals to reveal their presence to the bipeds. A polar bear, a whale, a dolphin, a sea lion, an elephant seal, a manatee, a narwhal—all would make the flipper signal, and Fred and sensitive bipeds like him would immediately know its significance, and, Daniel hoped, be astounded by such a collection of animals living together and joined to a single purpose. The bipeds would have to pay attention to the tribe, then, and in a way they had never done before.

Having convinced the bipeds of the intelligence and unusual degree of cooperation among the sea mammals, Daniel then planned to lead the bipeds and the tribe back into Pacifica. Once such sensitive beings as Fred saw the ruined caverns and figured out as Daniel had what had happened there, Daniel believed, they would understand a great deal more about the relationship of man and sea mammals. For Pacifica would show, in an indelible way, the terrible consequences of man's inability to accept that other forms of life had as much right to the oceans as man does. The darkest example would serve to illuminate its opposite, the path to the light, and from Pacifica bipeds would realize that sea mammals must never again be treated as less than equal inhabitants of the world.

There was difficult work ahead to convince bipeds to accept sea mammals as equals, but perhaps if that happened, bipeds and sea mammals all over the world might join together in tandem to save the seas.

Of course, the plan might not work. The bipeds could simply imprison the new tribe and lose the chance to save the world. But if Daniel did not risk approaching the bipeds, the likelihood was even greater that the oceans would soon be completely destroyed and that no sea mammals would survive to know their great-grandpups.

The shore loomed closer. Groups of individual bipeds turned and stared in the direction of the tribe. There was Fred; he had survived, and seemed to be waiting for the approach. Daniel au Fond took a deep breath, his fore-flippers touched sand, and he clambered out onto the land to begin the future.

Tom Shachtman is a documentary filmmaker, behavioral psychologist, playwright, and author. He has written award-winning programs for network and public television, as well as numerous books for children and adults.

Mr. Shachtman lives with his wife and two sons in New York City.